CHAPTER 1

Sophia stared blankly at the skyline, her long dark hair falling like a curtain over her shoulders. Carter Kane. Even his name irritated her, like a splinter she couldn't ignore. She was the last line of defense, and she wasn't about to let some smug businessman with too much charm and too little conscience tear it all down.

She eyed the perfectly stacked reports on her desk—everything in order, unlike the chaos in her head. Kane was coming, ready to sweet-talk the board and gut her company in the name of "efficiency."

She hated men like him—men who saw companies as trophies and people as pawns. Men who had no idea what it meant to build something worth protecting. Well, she wasn't going to let him win. Not today.

Sophia traced the folder, filled with every detail of Kane's tactics. Studying it only fueled her anger. Doubt nagged at her—what if she wasn't enough to save the company? Sophia shook her head sharply, as if to banish the thought. *Focus.*

Her father's portrait on the wall caught her eye, his stern, thoughtful face forever watching over her. She tucked a loose strand of dark hair behind her ear and straightened her shoulders, letting her big blue eyes linger on his image. "I won't fail you," she whispered, the words barely escaping her lips. "I won't let him destroy what you built."

She was her father's daughter. And no one—least of all Carter Kane—was going to take that from her.

Sophia's knuckles whitened around the folder as she reached for her phone, which instantly blared, slicing through the tense silence. Joshua—her lawyer.

She answered on the first ring, not bothering with pleasantries. "Joshua," she said, her voice tight. "What's the update?"

"Kane confirmed," Joshua said, his tone clipped. "He'll be at the board meeting today."

Of course Carter would be there—he never missed a chance to swoop in for the kill. "When did he confirm?" Her voice came out icier than she'd planned. Everything was slipping through her fingers, faster than she could grab it.

"This morning," Joshua replied. "Negotiations are moving faster than we thought. He's pushing for a complete restructuring of the company, and—" He hesitated.

"And what?" Sophia snapped, already knowing she wouldn't like the answer.

Joshua's voice lowered slightly, as if he didn't want to say it out loud. "Several board members are leaning toward his proposal. They're swayed by the idea of a more... aggressive strategy."

Sophia's anger flared, smoldering into a full blaze. Of course they were swayed—money always wins. Carter wasn't just any investor; he sold dreams of endless profit, no matter the cost to those who actually built things. People like her father.

"Let me guess," she muttered, pacing behind her desk. "He's promising them the world. Higher returns, bigger numbers, faster growth."

"Exactly," Joshua confirmed. "He's selling them a vision of a more profitable future, but it's all smoke and mirrors. You know how he operates. Kane's a shark, Sophia. He sees weakness, he strikes. Just be prepared."

Prepared. She was always prepared.

Prologue

*Carter Kane leaned back in his leather chair, his penthouse office bathed in the glow of the city lights. A headline flashed on his screen: "**Grant Technologies Unveils New Innovations, Set to Dominate the Industry.**"*

Grant Technologies. Carter's pulse quickened as the name clicked. James Grant. The man who had destroyed his father, leaving Richard Kane's reputation in ruins and his legacy in tatters. Carter had spent years rebuilding what little remained, but his father had been left with nothing.

Now, James Grant's company was thriving. But not for long.

Carter's lips curled into a cold smile. He would make them an offer they couldn't refuse. He'd dismantle Grant Technologies piece by piece, stripping it of anything that carried James Grant's signature. The company would be his, transformed and rebranded until no trace of the man who humiliated his father remained. Carter Kane would rise where Richard Kane fell, and the Grants would be left with nothing.

As he continued reading, one complication caught his eye: a new heir and CEO—Sophia Grant.

He shrugged it off. She was just another obstacle, and he was used to clearing those.

"Let the games begin," he muttered, reaching for his phone. It was time to take everything from them.

This time, there would be no mercy.

"He's not touching my father's company." Sophia bit out, her teeth grinding together. "He knows nothing about this place, about what it stands for."

Joshua's pause made her stomach knot. "Sophia, this isn't about what the company *was*. It's about what it's becoming. Sentiment won't win this fight."

She bristled at the implication. "I'm not losing this company, Joshua. Sentiment or otherwise."

"I know you won't," Joshua said, backpedaling. "Just... be ready. This is bigger than we anticipated."

"Let him bring his fight," Sophia growled. "I'll be ready."

They hung up, but Joshua's words stuck. *Be prepared.* As if she hadn't been preparing for this her whole life. She slammed the phone down, glaring at the documents. Kane was pushing a shiny new future, but he hadn't built this place. Grant Technologies was just another meal for him—consume, conquer, and leave the bones.

As she stared at the papers, the door to her office clicked open, and Jessica walked in, clipboard in hand.

"How are you feeling about the meeting?" Jessica asked, breezing in with her usual efficiency, yet there was an edge in her voice, a tightness in her posture.

"How do you think I'm feeling?" Sophia's voice was icier than she intended, but she didn't care. She could feel the pressure building, rising. She needed to let it out somewhere, and Jessica, of all people, should understand.

Jessica set the clipboard down, her fingers drumming the desk. "You've been killing it, Sophia," she said, eyes darting around like she wanted out. "But we can't keep this up forever. There's got to be a way to honor history without losing everything else— including you."

Sophia froze. Her eyes snapped to Jessica's face, searching for something. "What are you saying?"

Jessica's quick glance away was enough to spark doubt. "Look," she said, her tone now silky smooth, "fighting Kane nonstop isn't the only play. He's ruthless, sure, but he's powerful. Maybe there's a way to work *with* him—"

"Work with him?" Sophia's voice was low, incredulous. "You think I should let Carter Kane walk into my company and dictate its future? That's your advice?"

Jessica didn't flinch, but there was a quick flash in her eyes—resentment? Frustration? Gone in a blink. "Sometimes, fighting to the death isn't the only way to win." Her voice was calm, but Sophia wasn't buying it.

Sophia forced herself to stay cool, even as her temper flared.

Sophia approached the boardroom, her steps stable, her mind running through her strategy like a playlist on repeat. She'd faced these people plenty of times, but today the stakes were higher. She took a breath, easing her grip on the folder. It wasn't the doors that made her nervous—it was the familiar faces inside, once allies, now ready to question her every move.

She could see him now, strolling in with that cocky confidence, as if her company was already his. He'd dazzle them with promises of growth and profits, and some would fall for it. Some would believe his glittering vision.

The door opened, and the board members filed in. She didn't turn—couldn't show a hint of uncertainty. This was her meeting, and she was in control.

The shuffle of papers and quiet greetings barely registered as she ran through her points. Grant Technologies was about more than profits; it was about innovation and integrity. But as the last members took their seats, she felt a twist of distrust. Loyalty alone wouldn't cut it—not when profits sparkled like fool's gold.

And then she felt it—the shift in the room. Carter was here.

He took his seat across from her, unhurried and deliberate. The room fell silent, everyone waiting. He steepled his fingers, watching her, but she wasn't about to play his game.

"Let's begin," she said, slicing through the tension.

The meeting blurred with numbers and projections as Carter pitched his vision—rapid expansion, restructuring, doubling profits in half the time. Some board members nodded along, others glanced at Sophia, waiting for her take.

She stood firm, defending her father's core values. But she could see the apprehension creeping in—they were thinking about profits, not tradition.

Carter's smirk saying he thought he had it in the bag. But he hadn't factored in her resolve, the fire still burning inside her.

When the meeting ended, the tension lingered. The board wasn't ready to decide—they needed more time. Time Sophia wasn't sure she had.

She left the room, nerves buzzing. In the hallway, she paused to collect herself. She needed a plan—something strong enough to counter Carter's aggressive move and show the board she wasn't going to back down.

Taking a deep breath, she turned on her heel and headed for the office of Richard Blake, one of the more seasoned and pragmatic board members. Richard had been a close friend of her father's and had always offered no-nonsense advice. If there was anyone who could help her navigate this storm, it was him.

She knocked lightly and waited. After a moment, Richard's deep voice called out, "Come in."

She pushed open the door and stepped inside. Richard looked up from his papers, his shrewd eyes narrowing as he took in her tense expression.

"Sophia," he greeted her, setting his pen down. "You look like you've just come from the front lines. What's going on?"

She closed the door behind her, exhaling slowly. "Richard, I need your help."

He relaxed back in his chair, studying her carefully. "I figured as much. Is this about Carter Kane?"

She nodded, dropping the folder onto his desk. "He's gunning for us, Richard. He's trying to convince the board to go along with his ridiculous restructuring plan. Some of them are swayed by his promises of higher returns and bigger profits."

Richard frowned, flipping through the pages of the folder. "Typical. Kane's style has always been to dangle the prospect of a quick win. But we both know those gains come at a cost." He looked up, his gaze piercing. "What's your strategy?"

Sophia bit her lip, pacing in front of his desk. "That's why I'm here. I need something solid to counter his proposal. Something that doesn't just hold the line, but shows the board that we have a vision."

Richard nodded thoughtfully. "We need to remind them what Grant Technologies stands for. Your father always emphasized innovation and sustainable growth over quick profits. We have to reinforce that message." He paused, his eyes flicking to the portrait of her father on the wall. "Instead of getting into the specifics of any particular project, we should focus on the big picture. Show them that our long-term strategy isn't just about profit margins but about maintaining the integrity and values that built this company."

Sophia stopped pacing, considering his words. "So, we focus on the core principles? Highlight our track record and our commitment to innovation?"

"Exactly," Richard agreed. "Kane's tactics rely on undermining confidence in your leadership. We need to make it clear that not only do you have a solid vision for the future, but that it's rooted in principles that will ensure this company thrives for decades to come—not just until the next fiscal quarter."

Sophia nodded, the beginnings of a plan forming in her mind. "We need to play up our strengths—our stability, our ethical practices, our commitment to our employees and clients. Remind them why we've been successful for so long."

Richard smiled, a glimmer of pride in his eyes. "That's the spirit. You need to remind them why they believed in you, why they chose you to lead. And remember, the board wants to see strength. Show them you're not afraid to fight for this company."

Sophia's determination solidified, a surge of resolve flooding through her. "I will. And I'll need your support during the meeting. Can I count on you to back me up?"

"Of course," he said, his voice firm. "But Sophia, you need to be prepared for the possibility that not everyone will be on your side. Kane's good at what he does. He'll be expecting you to resist. We have to make sure we're one step ahead."

"I know," she murmured, already thinking through the next steps. "I'll prepare a comprehensive presentation that outlines our strategy and vision. We need to move fast before Carter has a chance to push his agenda any further."

Richard rose from his chair, coming around to place a reassuring hand on her shoulder. "You're doing great, Sophia. Your father would be proud of how you're handling this."

The words hit her hard, a bittersweet pang swelling in her chest. "Thanks, Richard. I just hope it's enough."

"It will be," he assured her. "Now go get to work. We've got a company to save."

Sophia gave him a grateful smile before turning and heading for the door.

CHAPTER 2

Carter's grip tightened around his coffee. The name Grant Technologies lingered like a bad aftertaste, his hazel eyes narrowing. He shifted in his chair, his broad shoulders tense with unfinished business.

It wasn't just business. Taking down the company that had destroyed his father would be the final piece of his revenge, the closure he'd craved for so long.

Leaning forward, he studied the reports. The numbers were clean, the path clear. Every step mapped out, yet the expected satisfaction eluded him.

This wasn't just another deal, Carter reminded himself. He would finish what should have been done years ago.

A knock at the door interrupted his thoughts. He didn't need to look up to know who it was. Eleanor had that uncanny ability to command a room just by entering it. Her determined hazel eyes—so like his own—missed nothing, and her short, perfectly styled hair only added to her no-nonsense demeanor.

"Carter," she greeted, her voice cutting through the room like the blade of a knife.

He glanced at her, raising a brow but staying silent. No surprise —Eleanor never waited for an invite. She strode in, eyes locked on his, all business.

"You spoke to the lawyers?" Carter asked, already knowing the answer.

"Everything's progressing," she replied, crossing her arms as she stood before him. "But I don't like the way you've been... hesitating."

His brow narrowed slightly. "I'm not hesitating."

Her lips tightened, irritation flashing briefly. "You're overthinking this. Remember why we're here, Carter. Remember what they did to us. To him."

The mention of their father hit hard, like always. "I haven't forgotten," Carter snapped. He didn't need reminders—he lived with that betrayal daily.

Eleanor's eyes drilled into him. "This isn't about profits," she said, her voice taut with the memory of their father's disgrace. "This is about taking back what was stolen. Our name. Our family. Don't let emotions cloud your judgment."

Carter felt that old surge of anger, not just at Eleanor, but at everything that had gone wrong. The headlines still haunted him: **"Richard Kane: A Business Buffoon?"** His father's face had been everywhere, dragged through the mud by every news outlet. They called him reckless, arrogant—a complete failure. What started as a bad deal spiraled into a full-blown disaster, with James Grant striking the match and the media pouring gasoline on the flames. Talk shows turned his dad into a joke, analysts picked apart his every move, and business columns practically celebrated his downfall.

Carter had gone to great lengths to scrub everything he could off the internet, burying articles and erasing videos, but it had taken monumental effort. It didn't matter, though—some stains were impossible to wash away.

Eleanor was right—this wasn't about the bottom line. This was about revenge. About justice.

Carter watched her retreat, his mind churning despite himself.

As she reached the door, she paused. "Stay focused, Carter. We're almost there."

His thoughts returned to the boardroom meeting earlier. He was accustomed to these battles, but something about today felt different. There was something about Sophia Grant that threw him.

She wasn't just tough—she was smart, fiercely protective of her family business, and impossible to intimidate. He respected that, maybe even admired it. And she was *stunning*—far more than he'd expected. But that didn't matter.

Attraction wouldn't distract him. She'd fall like the rest.

Carter turned from the window, reaching for his briefcase. It was just business, like all the other deals. Right?

CHAPTER 3

Sophia stepped out of the car, clutching her purse. It was Thursday happy hour, a weekly tradition for the Grant Technologies crew.

She scanned the cocktail lounge, spotting familiar faces. She needed to work the room, rally support, and keep her cool.

Taking a deep breath, she refocused. This was her chance to remind everyone why they believed in working for this company.

Then she saw him—Carter Kane. Her heart skipped, then pounded. He wasn't supposed to be here, but there he was, charming her crowd like he owned the place. He'd already taken over her boardroom; now he was crashing happy hour too?

She moved toward him, weaving through the crowd, tension building with every step. By the time she reached him, she was ready to blow.

"What are you doing here?" Her voice was low but sharp, her eyes blazing as they met his.

Carter turned, annoyingly calm. "Enjoying the evening?" he asked with a lazy smile. "Lovely event."

"You're gate-crashing, Kane. This is *my* happy hour, and you've got no business being here."

His smile stayed put. "But since I'm here, I plan to make the most of it."

"I know what you're up to. You think you can just waltz in and destroy everything? Not happening."

Carter's smile faded, a flash of something darker in his eyes. "I'm not here to wreck things. I'm trying to fix what you're too stuck in the past to see is falling apart."

Sophia stepped closer, voice low and fierce. "Fix it? By turning it into one of your corporate trophies? This isn't just a company— it's my family business, and I'm not letting you take it."

"Family business? The one the *great* James Grant built? That's not a legacy; it's a mess you're too blind to clean up." Carter threw her a cold smile and walked away before she could respond.

His words cut deep. Her dad was nothing like that—he was a great man, a visionary. How dare he say that!

"*I hate him,*" she told herself again, her chest lifting. "Why does he get under my skin like this?"

But no sooner had she put distance between them than Jessica appeared by her side. Her smile was polite, but her eyes didn't match it. They were distant, cool, as if she were watching from behind a wall.

"Everything okay?" Jessica asked, her tone casual, though it felt rehearsed.

"Fine," Sophia lied, still fuming from her confrontation with Carter. "Just... dealing with Kane."

Jessica raised an eyebrow, but her expression didn't change. "Don't let him get to you. He's not worth it. We need to stay focused on the big picture."

Her words were too casual, and it only added to Sophia's unease. With a thin smile, Jessica walked away, leaving Sophia rattled. What was up with Jessica? Her trusted COO seemed off.

Sophia's eyes swept over the happy hour crowd until she spotted

Carter, right in the middle of a group of sales managers. He was laughing, effortlessly charming, while the women around him looked like they were hanging on his every word. One even playfully touched his arm, and he didn't miss a beat, flashing that winning smile she was starting to hate.

Lipstick on a pig, she thought, biting back her frustration. How could they not see it? She wanted to deny he was attractive, but it was impossible to ignore—tall, handsome, and infuriatingly her type. It irritated her even more. *Why did he have to look like that?*

Just then, a perky voice broke through her thoughts. "Sophia! I just wanted to say how excited I am about the new direction the company is taking."

Sophia turned to see Erin from HR, all smiles and enthusiasm. Erin glanced over at Carter, her eyes practically sparkling.

"You mean *that* direction?" Sophia said, unable to keep the sarcasm out of her voice.

Erin giggled, clearly missing the bite in Sophia's words. "Yeah, I mean, look at him. He's so dynamic and confident! It's like he's breathing new life into the company."

Sophia forced herself to stay composed. "I guess 'new life' is one way to put it."

Erin pressed in a little closer, like she was sharing some juicy gossip. "I heard he's got big plans—streamlining, cutting the fat, really shaking things up. It's just what we need, don't you think?"

Sophia gave her a tight smile. "If by 'cutting the fat' you mean firing half the staff."

Erin blinked, caught off guard. "Oh, I'm sure it won't be that bad! I mean, he just seems so... passionate."

As Erin walked away, Sophia took another deep breath. She glanced back at Carter, who was now clinking glasses with the sales team, his smile gleaming under the bar lights. This was going to be tougher than she thought. Winning over the board was one thing, but getting the entire staff to see past his slick exterior?

This is going to be like climbing Everest in heels, she thought. But if anyone was up for the challenge, it was her.

CHAPTER 4

Carter reclined back in his car, city lights streaking by. Tom's message echoed in his mind: *David Grant. Buying shares.*

David? Unexpected, but interesting. Sophia had never mentioned her brother, not once. Odd for someone so fiercely protective of her family's business. If David was quietly buying in, why was that not disclosed? Maybe it wasn't just business—it was *personal*. And Carter knew personal motives were the most dangerous—and the most useful.

A plan started forming. Meeting with David could reveal weaknesses he could exploit. Maybe he could find leverage, something that would tip the balance in his favor. David wasn't just a curveball—it was an opportunity.

Carter shot off a quick text to his assistant: *Set up a discreet meeting with David Grant.*

Moments later, Tom's call came through. "Give me the details."

"David's been buying shares quietly, faster than expected. Staying under the radar but making moves," Tom reported, calm and precise.

"Seven percent?" Carter asked.

"Just under, and he's not stopping there. If you're planning a move, now's the time."

Carter drummed his fingers.

Tom chuckled. "She's clueless. Too focused on you to see her brother sneaking in."

A part of him— almost felt sorry for her. *Almost.*

Carter leaned back, the city sprawled beneath him like his personal empire. His penthouse office—high above it all—was a monument to his success, every sleek line and cutting-edge gadget broadcasted power. Yet, an itch of restlessness lingered, just beneath the surface.

Sophia Grant was proving to be a challenge, and he wasn't a man accustomed to being challenged. She was clever, passionate, and fiercely protective. But he couldn't afford to let admiration cloud his judgment. Not when he was so close to achieving what he'd set out to do.

"Keep tabs on David Grant's movements," he said, his voice thoughtful. "I want to know who he's talking to and what his next steps are. If he's planning something, we need to be ready."

"Already on it. But Carter, are you sure about this? Playing both sides—pitting Sophia against her brother—it's a dangerous game."

Carter's lips curved into a slow, confident smile. "It's only dangerous if you're not in control, Tom. And I always keep control." He ended his call with Tom and glanced at his phone, a sudden thought striking him.

He needed a break—a moment to clear his head and remind himself why he played this game. He dialed a number and waited, his fingers tapping lightly on the desk.

"Rosetti Imports, how can I help you today?" Came a smooth, professional voice.

"It's Carter Kane," he said, his tone casual but with an edge of authority that brooked no delay. "I'm calling to check on the status of my order."

"Ah, Mr. Kane! Of course. Let me pull that up for you," the voice replied, a hint of nervousness slipping through the professionalism. There was a brief pause, the sound of typing on a keyboard. "Yes, your Ferrari SF90 Spider has arrived, and it's currently being detailed. It should be ready for pickup by the end of the day."

"Excellent," Carter said, his mood lifting. "Make sure it's perfect. I'll be by this evening."

"Absolutely, sir. We'll have everything prepared."

He ended the call. There was something exhilarating about acquiring something new, something that few others could claim. The Ferrari, with its sleek lines and powerful engine, was a symbol of everything he'd built—a reminder that he played in a league of his own.

Carter hung up with Tom and immediately dialed his assistant. "Cancel my next meeting," he said as soon as she answered.

There was a brief pause. "Of course. What should I tell them?"

"Just say I'm otherwise engaged," he replied with a smirk. "I'll be back this evening."

She laughed softly. "Must be nice to take an afternoon off."

Carter grinned. "Perks of the job. You should try it sometime."

He shrugged on his jacket and headed out. He knew he was pushing hard—maybe harder than ever—but that was the thrill of it. The high stakes, the razor's edge between victory and defeat, the constant need to outdo himself. It made him feel alive, and he was addicted to that rush. He didn't dare slow down, didn't want to face whatever was waiting on the other side of that wall if he stopped chasing the next adrenaline high.

His driver was waiting with the car door open, and Carter slid into the back seat, the plush leather interior enveloping him in luxury. "Let's take the scenic route today," he said, his voice relaxed.

The driver nodded and pulled away from the curb, merging smoothly into traffic. As the car navigated through the streets, Carter's mind began to shift gears. He needed to think about his next move, how to keep the pressure on Sophia without overplaying his hand.

He pulled out his phone again and scrolled through his contacts, his eyes landing on the name of an old acquaintance —Jordan McAllister, a high-profile attorney who specialized in mergers and acquisitions. He was ruthless, confident and had a reputation for making deals happen, no matter the cost. Carter had used him before, and Jordan's involvement always sent a clear message: he meant business.

He tapped the name, waiting as the phone rang.

"McAllister," came the curt response.

"Jordan, it's Carter Kane. I need you to confirm a hunch for me. It's urgent."

There was a pause before Jordan's voice turned smooth and professional. "What are we looking at?"

"I think David's buying up shares, hoping for a big payout to settle debts. I need confirmation."

Jordan let out a low whistle. "Risky move, but if he's desperate enough... I'll dig into his finances and share purchases. If there's something to it, you'll know."

"Perfect," Carter said, his voice crisp and controlled. "I need the details on my desk by tomorrow."

"On it," Jordan replied. "I'll get my team right on this."

The car pulled up in front of the dealership, and Carter stepped out, his stare locking on the gleaming red Ferrari waiting for him. It was beautiful—glossy, powerful, and utterly unattainable for most people. Just the way he liked it.

He ran a hand over the smooth, polished surface.

"Mr. Kane, your vehicle is ready," the dealership manager said, beaming with pride. "I trust everything is to your satisfaction?"

"Absolutely," Carter replied, his smile widening. "It's perfect."

He slid into the driver's seat, the leather molding to his form as if it had been custom-made just for him. The engine purred to life with a low growl, and Carter felt a thrill rush through him. He glanced at the dealership manager, giving him a nod of approval before revving the engine and pulling out onto the street.

The car surged forward, the power beneath him exhilarating. As he roared down the boulevard, Carter felt that familiar surge of adrenaline. This was what he lived for—the speed, the power, the sense that he was unstoppable.

He tore down the open road, weaving through traffic with ease. The car handled like a dream, every turn and acceleration perfectly in tune with his movements. It was pure freedom, pure control. And for those precious minutes, he let everything else fall away—the deal, Sophia, David, and the tension of the past weeks. All that mattered was the road and the machine beneath him.

But as he sped past the city limits, his mind inevitably drifted back to the game he was playing. The stakes were high, and the board was still on the fence. He needed to show them that he was the only one who could take Grant Technologies to the next level, the only one who had the vision and the power to make the hard decisions.

With a final burst of speed, he pushed the Ferrari to its limits, the roar of the engine echoing in his ears like a battle cry.

This was his world. And he was about to remind everyone exactly who ruled it.

CHAPTER 5

Sophia stepped out of the office to grab a salad, starving. Her legal advisor never called casually. Her stomach knotted—this wasn't going to be good.

"Hey Joshua, what's up?" she answered her cell, voice tense.

After a pause, Joshua spoke. "Sophia, I dug into those shares you asked about after Accounting flagged them. It's definitely suspicious."

Her grip tightened. "Who?"

"David."

Sophia felt as though the ground had disappeared beneath her feet. David? Her brother, who had shown zero interest in the company, had taken a position for all of five minutes, and then bailed at the first sign of trouble because it wasn't his "cup of tea," was now buying shares? He left years ago, what the hell?

"David's buying shares?" she whispered, shock mixing with rising anger.

"Yes," Joshua said, serious. "He's been at it for months, using proxies to stay hidden. But it's definitely him."

Sophia's grip tightened on her phone. "I have to go," she said abruptly, her mind running wild. "Thanks, Joshua."

She ended the call and immediately dialed her mom. It rang twice before the familiar, warm voice answered.

"Sophia! Sweetheart, how are you? Did you get the cookies I sent last week?"

"Hi, Mom. Yes, I did. They were delicious, thank you." She forced a smile into her voice but didn't waste time. "Listen, I need to ask —what's going on with David lately?"

There was a pause, then her mom's voice softened. "David? Honey, you haven't asked about him in years. What brought this on?"

Sophia took a deep breath, trying to keep her tone casual. "Just curious. Anything new with him?"

"Well, he's been going through a rough patch after the divorce," her mom said, her voice heavy with concern. "He's trying to bounce back. I think he's seeing someone new, but he doesn't talk about it much. Other than that, same old David. Why, what's this about?"

Sophia's heart sank. David was hurting, but he was still making moves against her, against the company. "No reason, just wondering," she said, trying to sound breezy. "You know, making sure he's okay."

Her mom let out a small sigh. "He's hanging in there. I wish you two would talk."

"Yeah, maybe we will," Sophia said. "Thanks, Mom. I'll call you later, okay?"

"Of course, sweetheart. Take care of yourself."

"You too, Mom." Sophia hung up, staring at her phone, her mind spinning. David was more than just okay—he was plotting.

As she tried to ground herself, her phone lit up. She glanced down to see a message from Evan, her ex-boyfriend: *Lunch today?* She rolled her eyes. *Seriously?* No. Not today. *Not ever.*

Reopening that chapter was the last thing she needed. Evan was part of a mess she'd worked hard to clean up, and she wasn't about to dive back into *that* emotional chaos.

She shoved her phone back into her bag and took a deep breath, grabbing her salad and pushing through the revolving doors. Inside, Carter strolled through the lobby, phone to his ear, radiating his usual smug confidence. He looked like he owned the place—which, knowing him, he probably thought he did.

Arrogant jerk, she fumed, watching a couple of women by the elevators giggle and gawk at him. Did no one see he was just a polished vulture, circling her company?

She brushed past them, ignoring the whispers, her mind in overdrive between David and Carter. This day was spiraling fast.

The rest of the day was a blur. She barely registered the elevator ride down to the parking garage, her thoughts tangled in a chaotic mess of family betrayal and boardroom battles.

Sophia slid into the driver's seat of her car and sat for a moment. She needed to get a grip—needed to think. But right now, she just needed to get out of here.

She started the car and pulled out of the garage, heading towards home. Her phone chimed with another email notification, but she ignored it. Her inbox was full of requests, demands, and questions—everyone needing *something* from her. And that was the problem. She was always the one holding everything together, always the one in control. But today felt different. Today, it felt like everything was slipping.

She reached her townhouse, a modern, minimalist structure. She tossed her bag onto the marble countertop and kicked off her shoes, the tension in her shoulders refusing to ease. The house was immaculate, as always. No sign of life, no clutter—just like her schedule demanded. Everything in its place, every surface pristine. It was a reflection of her life: orderly, controlled, and utterly devoid of warmth.

Sophia collapsed onto the couch, eyes on the framed photo of her father. His smile, equal parts stern and proud, brought back memories of the day they'd landed their first big deal. Fresh out of college, she'd been desperate to prove she was more than just the boss's daughter.

Her chest tightened as memories rushed in. Those early days were electric—working side by side, building something real. She'd traded nights out for all-nighters at the office, sacrificed relationships to chase dreams. When he died, her world turned grayscale, reduced to contracts and board meetings.

She bent forward, elbows on her knees, burying her face in her hands. She'd built her life around the company, poured herself into every decision, every deal. But what did she have to show for it? An empty house, an inbox full of unread emails, and the constant, gnawing pressure to be *perfect*.

Her phone buzzed again, and she glanced at it reluctantly. An email from Jessica, her COO and supposed friend. *Need to discuss the board's reaction to Kane's proposal. Can you meet early tomorrow?* Even Jessica had seemed distant lately, her once-supportive attitude replaced by a cold professionalism that put Sophia on edge. Was there anyone left she could trust?

With a sigh, she tossed the phone aside and stood, wandering into the kitchen. She pulled a bottle of wine from the cooler and poured herself a glass, watching the deep red liquid swirl in the crystal. She rarely drank—too much work, too many responsibilities. But this week, she needed something to take the edge off, something to quiet the noise in her head.

She carried the glass back to the living room and sat down again. She was a success, *wasn't she*? A powerhouse in the industry, the CEO of a multimillion-dollar company. But as she sat there, alone in the pristine silence of her perfect home, she couldn't shake the feeling that it wasn't enough. That maybe, just maybe, she'd given up too much along the way.

She took a sip of wine, the bitter taste grounding her. This was her life—work, an empty house, and more work. She couldn't remember the last time she'd done something just for herself. A dinner that wasn't with a client, a vacation that wasn't cut short by some crisis at the office. Even her attempts at dating felt like items to check off a list, something to fit into her schedule between board meetings and investor calls.

Sophia sank into the couch, eyes closed. This wasn't just tired —it was the kind of bone-deep exhaustion that came from keeping everything and everyone in check, day in and day out. Always the one in control, even as she felt herself unraveling. Every crisis managed, every decision made, chipped away at her, leaving her more frayed by the day.

The thought of going to bed, only to wake up and do it all over again, was almost unbearable. But what else was there? She didn't know how to stop, didn't know how to be anything other than this driven, relentless version of herself.

She took another sip of wine and glanced back at the photo on the wall, her father's eyes seeming to watch her, as if judging her choices. "What would you do, Dad?" she whispered, her voice breaking. "What am I supposed to do now?"

CHAPTER 6

Carter glanced up from his phone and spotted a striking woman across the lobby. Women were never a problem—they usually threw themselves at him. Then he realized: it was Sophia, holding a sad little salad. She wasn't the type of pretty that was easy or approachable. She was all sharp edges—a challenge, not a conquest.

His plan was simple: use David's greed to take down his sister. But was it really that simple?

As he passed her, she didn't even look up. That stung more than it should've. Women always noticed him. Why did it bug him that she didn't?

He pushed it aside and refocused. He had a discreet meeting with David on the 4th floor. David was too eager to meet—definitely a red flag. The guy had *desperation* written all over him.

Carter stepped into the elevator, watching as the doors closed on Sophia, who didn't even glance his way. Damn, she'd be tougher to crack than he thought.

He stepped out of the elevator on the 4th floor, his mind already calculating. David's eagerness was a neon sign flashing *danger*. But he was useful—*for now*.

David was waiting in a small conference room, pacing. When Carter walked in, he stopped and shot him a tight smile. "Glad you could make it."

"Of course," Carter said smoothly, taking a seat and motioning for David to do the same. "I hear you've been busy."

David leaned forward, excitement barely contained. "I've been buying up shares. Quietly. Once I have enough, I'll have the majority vote, and I can push Sophia out as CEO."

Carter arched an eyebrow. "And you think you can pull that off?"

David's smile widened. "This company should be mine, not hers. If investors are circling, then she's obviously not doing her job. I mean, why else would you be coming in? I should be the one in charge." His voice was laced with resentment. "And if it means merging with Carter Enterprises to get it done, then I'm in."

Really? The name was *Kane* Enterprises, not *Carter* Enterprises. If this guy couldn't even get the name right then maybe this guy wasn't the brightest. Carter didn't correct him. The truth was, Grant Technologies wasn't in financial trouble—he'd singled them out for personal reasons, not because of any fiscal weakness. But David didn't need to know that.

"I want her out," David continued, eyes blazing. "Whatever it takes. I can get the board to vote her off. They trust me, or they will once they see the numbers."

Carter nodded, keeping his expression neutral. "And in exchange, you'd merge with *Carter Enterprises*, with you as the new CEO?"

David's grin was almost predatory. "Exactly. You'll get what you want, and I'll finally have what's *mine*."

Carter tilted back, pretending to consider it. David was more desperate than he'd thought, and desperation could be useful. But one misstep and this alliance could backfire spectacularly. Still, he gave a small nod, as if weighing his options.

"Let's see how things play out," Carter said finally. "We're both after the same goal. If you can get the board on your side, then we'll talk *next steps*."

David nodded, his eyes gleaming. "I won't let you down."

Carter stood, extending his hand. "Then let's keep this between us for now. It's going to take careful planning to make this work."

"Agreed," David said, shaking his hand firmly. His smile was confident, but there was a tension in his eyes, a flicker of anxiety that Carter couldn't ignore. As David turned and walked out of the office, Carter felt a prickle of unease crawl up his spine.

Barely a minute after the door closed behind David, Carter's phone beeped with a notification. He glanced at the screen—McAllister. He swiped to answer.

"What do you have for me?" he asked, his voice low and direct.

"Your hunch was right," McAllister replied without preamble. "David's in over his head. He's been buying up shares using cash from some pretty shady sources. Loan sharks, to be specific."

Carter's jaw tightened. "How deep is he?"

"Deep enough that he's desperate for a big payoff. If he doesn't get the money soon, his creditors are going to come knocking —and these aren't the kind of people who take late payments lightly. We're talking about serious players, Carter. The kind who don't mind breaking a few bones to get what they're owed."

Carter swore under his breath. "Damn it, David. So he's betting everything on this deal going through."

"Exactly. If he can flip those shares for a big payout, he might just scrape by. But if not... let's just say, his problems are going to get a lot more dangerous."

Carter ran a hand through his hair, thinking fast. "And there's no way he can pull out without losing everything?"

"Not a chance. He's locked in. If the deal falls apart, so does he."

Carter let out a slow breath, his mind already shifting gears. David wasn't just a loose cannon—he was a loaded one, and if he exploded, it could blow up everything Carter had been working for.

"Thanks, Jordan. Keep this under wraps. I'll handle it."

"Will do," McAllister said, his tone serious. "And Carter? Watch your back. These guys don't play around."

"I'll keep that in mind," Carter replied, his voice steely. He hung up and shifted back in his chair, staring at the closed door where David had just walked out.

David was in way over his head, and putting him in any position of power would be a disaster waiting to happen. Carter couldn't risk that kind of liability. Yes, he was here to erase any trace of James Grant from the company, but once he took it over, it would still be his. He didn't build a billion-dollar empire by making foolish business decisions, and David was exactly that— a mistake.

CHAPTER 7

Sophia pushed open the door to her townhouse, the soft click of the lock echoing in the too-quiet space. She lingered for a moment, hand still on the doorknob, as if staying there could keep the chaos of the day from spilling in. But it couldn't. Her grip on control was slipping, and she knew it.

She sat at her kitchen table, a glass of untouched wine beside her, flipping through the ruthless takeover proposal from Kane Enterprises. Cut half the staff, change the name, scrap employee protections—it was like they wanted to erase every trace of her father.

Why her company? Profits were good—not record-breaking, but stable. The employees were happy. There was no glaring weakness, no reason for him to have approached the firm like he was saving it from financial disaster. So why this aggressive push to take over? And why insist on stripping away everything that made Grant Technologies unique? Something wasn't sitting well.

She couldn't ignore it, though. The board had seen Carter's shiny projections and were intrigued. He'd dangled the promise of high returns, and now they were curious, if not outright tempted. Nothing was final yet, but the fact that they were even entertaining the idea was unsettling. Did they really have to change the name and butcher what her father had built?

The thought made her sick. She pushed the papers away trying to clear her mind. The doorbell rang, breaking her from her thoughts. She took a deep breath, then went to open the door for

Jessica.

"Hey," Sophia greeted, stepping back to let her in. "Thanks for coming."

"Of course," Jessica said, shrugging off her coat and glancing at the scattered papers. "Rough day?"

"You could say that," Sophia replied, pouring Jessica a glass of wine. "I've been trying to figure out why Carter's coming at us so hard. Profits are good, people are happy... Why now?"

Jessica took the glass, her eyes scanning the documents. "Maybe he just sees potential. A good company he can make great."

"By tearing it apart?" Sophia asked, frustration boiling over. "Why insist on changing the name and firing half the staff? It's like they want to wipe us out."

Jessica hesitated, then took a sip of wine. "Maybe he doesn't care about the history. Just sees it as a stepping stone."

Sophia shook her head. "I'm not just going to roll over and let him destroy everything we've built."

Jessica nodded, but before she could respond, Sophia blurted out, "And there's more. I found out David's been buying up shares."

"David—*your brother*?" Jessica's eyes widened before she quickly masked her surprise. "Why would he do that?"

"That's what I'm trying to figure out," Sophia said, pacing the room. "He's using proxies to keep his name hidden. What's his endgame? He walked away from the company years ago."

Jessica's expression turned guarded. "Maybe he just wants back in."

"Why now, though? It doesn't make sense." Sophia stopped pacing and looked at Jessica, frustration in her voice. "Do you know anything about this?"

She shook her head, a little too quickly. "No, nothing. I'm as surprised as you are."

Sophia studied her friend for a moment, then sighed. "I just don't get it. And it's not just David—it's the board, too. They're all suddenly listening to Carter, and I can't shake the feeling that I'm missing something."

Jessica glanced down. "You'll figure it out. You always do."

Sophia let out a dry laugh. "I hope so. Because if I don't, there might be nothing left."

Jessica forced a smile, but something felt off. As the silence stretched, doubt crept in. David's scheming, the board's indecision, and now Jessica's distance—it was like the ground was shifting under her feet.

CHAPTER 8

The bold knock on the door jolted Carter from his thoughts, and before he could respond, the door swung open. Eleanor, his ever punctual sister, strode in with her usual no-nonsense stride. Her eyes swept the room before locking onto him, suspicion pulling at her features.

"What's this about?" she demanded, her tone clipped.

Carter reclined back, arms crossed. "We have leverage to shift the board—David Grant, Sophia's brother. But he's a *huge* liability."

Eleanor's eyes lit up, leaning forward. "David? *Interesting.* How can we use him?"

"That's the problem," Carter said, his tone purposeful. "He's been quietly buying shares, thinking he can influence the board. But putting him in any position of power would be a disaster. He's reckless and unpredictable."

Eleanor nodded, missing the point. "If he can sway the board, the deal's as good as done."

Carter's frown deepened. "You're not listening. This guy is a ticking time bomb. We can't afford to rely on him."

Eleanor's eyes gleamed as she inclined forward. "We don't have the board right now. If David can sway them, we have a deal. And without a deal, who cares who the CEO is?"

"That's the issue," Carter shot back. "Throwing a new CEO into the mix who doesn't know the business? It'll backfire on us later."

Eleanor waved off his concerns. "We'll worry about that later. Right now, we need the board."

She wasn't wrong—they needed the board's support to seal the deal. But once the company was his, it had to be profitable, and David seemed reckless. Replacing the CEO now would create instability and could jeopardize the entire takeover. At least Sophia knew the business and could keep things reliable during the transition.

"Eleanor, listen," Carter said firmly. "Changing CEO's right now would create chaos and could jeopardize everything. We need stability to secure the board's support. David's unpredictable behavior would only lead to bigger problems—both now and down the line."

Eleanor didn't even look back as she left. "Just get it done, Carter."

He watched the door close, a flicker of regret surfacing. He was used to running his own deals, making his own calls. Bringing Eleanor in after she got laid off was meant to be a favor, but maybe it wasn't the best move. Her personal vendetta against the Grants made her eager, but also impulsive.

He would deal with Eleanor later. Right now, he needed more intel on Sophia—maybe even a way to get her on his side. For now, she was the best option to keep things consistent.

He pulled out his laptop and started digging. *Sophia Grant.* Impressive résumé, stellar LinkedIn profile, charity board member. *Practically a saint.*

He typed in *David Grant* next. Not much came up—just some recent records of a nasty divorce. Apparently, he'd cheated. It was in the fine print, but Carter was good at finding small details. He hated that kind of behavior. It gave men a bad name. Sure, he had a reputation as a playboy, but he never made commitments he couldn't keep. He wouldn't be *that* guy. If he found the right woman, though, he'd commit. Someone strong and independent, who didn't need his money or his name.

He fired off a text to his assistant: *Find out if Sophia's free for lunch. Make it happen.*

CHAPTER 9

Sophia stepped into the restaurant, her eyes sweeping the room. Carter was already there, sitting in a dimly lit corner, exuding his usual air of control. She hadn't expected his assistant to schedule lunch. She'd been tempted to say no, but refusing him might send the wrong message to the board. As she approached the table, the thought nagged at her: Was this a smart move, or a mistake?

He glanced up as she neared, rising slightly from his seat. His eyes locked onto hers with that unreadable stare he always had.

"Sophia," he greeted, his voice smooth but with an edge beneath the charm.

She sat down, her back straight, pulse quickening despite herself. "Carter," she replied evenly, though her heart still raced from the moment she'd walked in.

"Busy day?" he asked casually, his smile easy. "I imagine running a company keeps you on your toes."

She raised an eyebrow. "Cut to the chase, Carter. Why are we here?"

He slouched back, hands spread in mock surrender. "I thought it'd be good to get to know the woman who's going to be the new CEO of... *Pinnacle Systems.*"

Sophia's eyes flashed with anger. "Pinnacle Systems? You're delusional. You can't just change the name. And you can't cut jobs like it's nothing."

Carter stayed calm. "Sophia, this is more than just business.

You're passionate, and I respect that. But I think you're missing the bigger picture."

"What bigger picture?" she shot back, her frustration mounting. "Why did you go after us? Profits are good, people are happy—why go after Grant Technologies?"

He studied her for a moment, then edged forward slightly. "You know our dads knew each other, don't you?"

Sophia's eyes narrowed. "Seriously? Our dad's? I don't know anything about your dad, but I'm guessing they were *worlds* apart."

Carter's jaw tightened, a flicker of anger crossing his face. "You *sure* about that?"

Before she could respond, the waitress appeared at their table, a bright smile plastered on her face. "Hi there! Can I get you both something to drink?"

Carter's demeanor shifted instantly, the tension melting away as he turned on the charm. "Of course. I'll have an old fashioned, and for the lady..." He glanced at Sophia.

"Just water," she said curtly, barely hiding her irritation.

The waitress nodded, jotting it down. "And by the way, there's a sweet little old lady here who says she knows you," she added, looking at Carter.

Carter blinked, surprised. "Okay...?"

The waitress gestured, and a tiny woman with a warm smile shuffled over, her eyes lighting up when she saw Carter. "There's the man who helped me!" she exclaimed.

Recognition dawned on Carter's face. He stood up and gave her a gentle hug. "Mrs. Mendez! How are you? Feeling better?"

Sophia watched, her irritation giving way to confusion.

"Oh, much better, dear, thanks to you!" Mrs. Mendez said, patting his arm. "This gentleman here," she said, turning to the waitress and Sophia, "saw me pass out in the coffee line down the street. It was my blood pressure! He didn't just call an ambulance—he personally took me to the hospital and stayed with me until my daughter arrived."

Sophia's eyebrows shot up as the waitress beamed.

Carter shrugged with a humble smile. "Just glad you're okay, Mrs. Mendez.

"You're a good man. Don't let anyone tell you otherwise."

Sophia, caught off guard, shifted in her seat. "So, uh, what was that about?"

Carter laughed, leaning back. "See? I'm not a terrible person."

She smirked. "Well, isn't *that* convenient."

The waitress returned with his old fashioned, and Sophia, feeling her guard drop just a bit, sighed. "Fine, I'll have a glass of wine."

"Wine, huh?" Carter raised an eyebrow.

Sophia shrugged, forcing a casual smile. "Yeah, it's been a week."

He leaned back, a playful glint in his eyes. "Ever tried Barolo? I swear, there's nothing like a good Italian wine to take the edge off."

She blinked, genuinely surprised. "Barolo? That's actually my favorite." Her tone softened, almost involuntarily. "I wouldn't have pegged you as a wine guy."

He grinned. "There's a lot you don't know about me."

Sophia couldn't help but laugh, a little of the tension easing. "Apparently. So, do you have a favorite region, or are you just a general wine enthusiast?"

He swirled his glass thoughtfully. "I've got a soft spot for Piedmont. Spent some time there a few years back. Fell in love with the place—and the wine, obviously."

"Really?" She realized she was leaning in, drawn in by his easy charm and annoyingly good looks. Irritated with herself, she tried to put her guard back up. "I've always wanted to visit."

"Add it to your list," he said, his voice dropping to a conspiratorial whisper. "And make sure to stop by a little family-owned vineyard called Cascina Adelaide. Their Barolo is out of this world."

Sophia shook her head, almost smiling. "Who knew Carter Kane was a secret wine connoisseur?"

He chuckled. "Like I said, there's more to me than corporate takeovers."

"Still trying to figure out if that's true," she teased lightly.

The wine had begun to loosen the edges of Sophia's nerves, and for a brief, surreal moment, she almost forgot she was sitting across from her sworn enemy. As they traded stories, the lines between rivalry and curiosity blurred. She found herself talking about that summer in the Swiss Alps when she'd nearly given up, lost and alone in the wilderness.

"I was convinced I'd be another 'tourist gone missing' headline," she confessed, shaking her head. "I kept thinking, 'This is it, I'm going to be found frozen on some cliffside, clutching a half-eaten protein bar.'"

Carter chuckled, his eyes holding hers with a new warmth. "But you made it out. Somehow, I'm not surprised."

"Barely," she said, the memory of that night still vivid. "Probably the stupidest thing I've ever done." *Why am I sharing this?* She thought. It felt so easy to talk to him, *too easy.* She should have been on guard, remembering who he was.

His face softened, the competitive edge melting away. "I don't think it was stupid at all. You're stronger than I gave you credit for."

Sophia raised an eyebrow. "You've been underestimating me, Mr. Kane?"

He smirked, leaning back in his chair. "Guilty as charged. I've never had to rely on anyone but myself. Maybe that's why I push so hard—sometimes too hard."

The air between them shifted, tension melting into something warmer. She kept getting pulled in by those damn eyes, her guard slipping every time she looked at him. *This was dangerous.*

Sophia tilted her head, forcing a casual tone as she tried to steer the conversation and rebuild her defenses. "So, if you push yourself that hard, what do you do to unwind?"

"Unwind?" Carter's smile turned playful. "I'm not sure I know the meaning of the word."

"Oh, come on. Everyone has something," she insisted. "Some people take up yoga or, I don't know, paint or—"

"Jump out of airplanes?" he offered casually.

She blinked, caught off guard. "Skydiving? You actually do that?"

"A few times, actually," he said, a mischievous glint lighting up his face. "It's the only thing that clears my head. What about you?"

She laughed, shaking her head. "Nope. *Never.* Not interested."

His smile widened. "Scared? I don't believe it."

"Terrified," she admitted, leaning in as if sharing a secret. A playful smile tugged at her lips before she could stop herself. "Maybe you're not so bad, Kane." The words slipped out, and she instantly regretted it. What was she thinking? She shouldn't be letting her guard down, shouldn't be letting his charm get to her.

"Don't let it get around," he said, leaning closer, his tone conspiratorial. "I've got a reputation to maintain."

Then her phone chirped with a text from Joshua, her lawyer. *Sophia, I reviewed the latest documents and found some language about asset liquidation buried in the fine print. We need to go over this ASAP. Call me.*

The words hit her like a splash of cold water. Asset liquidation? She glanced back at Carter, who was watching her with a relaxed smile, seemingly unaware of the bombshell that had just dropped.

Sophia's stomach twisted. *What was she doing?* She couldn't be sitting here, trading travel stories with the man trying to gut her entire company.

She slipped her phone back into her bag, forcing herself to straighten. "I should go," she said abruptly, the warmth that had been building between them evaporating in an instant.

Carter's brow furrowed, clearly sensing the shift. "Everything okay?"

"Just business," she replied, her tone cool again. "Something's come up that I need to deal with."

He nodded, but there was a flicker of something in his eyes—curiosity, maybe, or suspicion. "Right. Duty calls."

CHAPTER 10

Carter felt the shift instantly as Sophia rushed off, leaving him sitting there with half a burger and her barely-touched salad. The easy flow of their conversation had disappeared, replaced by the cold reality of why they were there in the first place.

He signaled the waitress. "Can I get this to go, please?" he asked, nodding at his plate. He paid the bill, slipping a generous tip under the edge of the check, then pulled out his phone to find a text from an old flame, Sarah. Beautiful, sexy, and always up for a good time. Normally, he'd be tempted to reply, but tonight, he couldn't muster any interest. Odd.

Ignoring the message, he headed home to his sprawling, empty house. He tossed his keys on the counter, the echo of silence making the place feel even more hollow. The thrill of his new car purchase was already fading. With a sigh, he switched on the sports channel and sank onto the couch, but his mind kept drifting back to Sophia.

She clearly had her act together. That much was obvious. In all her stories, she'd never once mentioned her brother, and she seemed genuinely oblivious about their fathers' connection. Was she telling the truth? If her dad had ruined his, wouldn't she know? She hadn't acted like someone hiding a family secret.

He glanced at his phone again, this time opening his messages to find an unread one from the retirement home. It had been a while since he'd visited his dad, and guilt twisted in his gut. Without overthinking it, he grabbed his coat and headed out the door.

The nursing home was quiet, the antiseptic smell familiar and jarring. He found his father in the small, cluttered room, staring blankly at a television that wasn't even turned on. Carter's heart clenched at the sight. His father, once a formidable presence, now looked frail and lost, a shadow of the man he'd been.

"Hey, Dad," Carter said softly, pulling up a chair beside the bed.

His father turned slowly, eyes vacant. "Do I know you?"

"It's me, Carter. Your son," he said, trying to keep his voice unchanging.

"Oh," his father murmured, his eyes drifting away. "Carter... yeah."

Carter swallowed hard, then tried again. "Dad, do you remember James Grant? What happened between you two?"

His father's expression shifted, but it was hard to tell if it was recognition or just confusion. "James... James Grant," he muttered, and for a moment Carter thought he might get something coherent. But then his father's eyes glazed over again, and he said, "You know, I used to love the apple pie at that diner on Fifth Street. Best in the city."

Carter's heart sank. He knew the signs—the conversation had slipped away. "Yeah, Dad, the pie was great," he said softly, forcing a smile.

His father chuckled, his mind wandering somewhere else entirely. "And the waitress, what was her name? Mary? Always gave me extra whipped cream."

Carter nodded, his throat tight. "Yeah, Mary."

He stayed for a while longer, listening to his dad ramble about people and places that didn't matter anymore. As he stood to leave, his father looked up, a flicker of clarity in his eyes.

"Are you okay, son?" he asked.

Carter froze, taken aback by the sudden lucidity. "Dad?"

His father's eyes seemed to clear for just a moment. "Remember the boat, Carter? We used to fish on Saturdays. Best days of my life... What was the name of that lake?"

Carter's heart sank.

But his dad was already slipping away, lost in a faded memory. Carter's shoulders slumped, the brief spark of hope snuffed out as quickly as it had appeared.

He left the room quietly, the empty corridors of the nursing home echoing his footsteps. Outside, the cold air hit him, cold and sobering. He glanced back at the building, his resolve unraveling.

As a child, he used to think his father was invincible, a giant who could do no wrong. They'd spent hours at the lake, his father teaching him to fish, laughing whenever he fumbled with the rod. 'Keep trying, son,' he'd say. 'You'll get it.' It was one of the few times Carter felt truly seen, truly loved.

But those moments seemed like a lifetime ago, drowned out by the years of bitterness and anger that followed. Now, looking back at the nursing home, he wondered if revenge would ever be enough to fill the hollow space where his father's approval used to be. *Cars weren't filling that hole either*, he realized. *Expensive realization.*

He pulled out his phone and called Eleanor. "You should go check on Dad soon," he said, trying to keep his voice unwavering.

"I saw him a few days ago," she replied, her tone heavy. "It's getting too hard, Carter. He's just... not there anymore."

There was a pause, a sadness in her voice that he rarely heard. "It kills me that he won't be at the wedding," she continued, her voice breaking slightly. "He's supposed to walk me down the aisle."

"I'll do it," Carter said softly. "I'll walk you down the aisle."

There was a silence, then she whispered, "Thanks, Carter. I have to go. I'm meeting with David tonight. We're moving forward with our plans."

"We don't *have* plans with David, Eleanor."

"Yes, *we do*," she said, her voice steely. "We do *now*." And with that, she hung up.

Carter stared at the phone, a cold knot forming in his stomach. Eleanor was moving forward without him, and with David of all people. Shit. That was not the plan.

A sharp sound emanated from his phone again, and he glanced down at a text from Blake. *Hey, man, I'm here. Are you close?*

Damn. He'd completely forgotten about dinner. They'd made plans weeks ago, and Blake was already at the restaurant. He let out a frustrated breath, shoving his phone back into his pocket and heading to his truck. A brand new car in the garage and yet he was still driving the *truck*.

On my way.

"Damn, you look like hell." His buddy said as Carter slipped into the booth.

"Thanks for the confidence boost," Carter muttered, picking up his water glass, though he didn't drink from it.

Blake shrugged, "You know me. Always here to keep you grounded. But seriously, man. You've been off the last few times we've met. Something going on at work?"

Carter's fingers tightened around the glass, the memory of Sophia hitting him. Why couldn't he focus?

"Just business," he said finally, forcing the words out as if they didn't leave a bitter taste in his mouth.

Blake shot him a sideways glance. "Yeah? Business, huh? Must be a big deal if it's messing with your head."

Carter set his glass down, leaning back in his chair and rubbing a hand over his jaw. He didn't usually open up, even with Blake. But Blake had this way of knowing things—of getting under his skin when Carter least wanted it.

"There's someone I've been dealing with," Carter said slowly, testing the waters. "Let's just say, she's... complicated."

Blake raised an eyebrow, looking intrigued. "*She*? Now this is interesting. You're telling me this is about a woman? Man, I thought you were just overworked. Didn't think you even had time for women these days."

"Not like that," Carter shot back, though he wasn't even sure if he believed his own words. "It's... business-related. She's the CEO of a company I'm working to acquire."

Blake gave him a look that said he wasn't buying it. "You've never let a business deal rattle you."

"It's not that," he pleaded, the words coming out before he could stop them.

Blake reclined back in his chair, crossing his arms as a slow grin spread across his face. "Oh, man. You've got it bad."

Carter scowled. "It's not like that."

Blake's expression softened. "Something on your mind?"

"I don't know, I've just been thinking a lot lately..." Carter trailed off, rubbing the back of his neck. Maybe the visits with his dad were getting to him more than he realized. Carter laughed. "I'm starting to wonder what else is out there beyond power plays and boardroom wars."

Blake shifted, still looking stunned. "Who are you and what have you done with Carter? Of course there's more to life than money

BILLIONAIRE IN THE BOARDROOM

and power."

"Like what?" Carter asked, genuinely curious.

"Like being a good person, helping others... Maybe you need to find yourself a *woman*, Carter," Blake said with a grin. "Have a family. I know you've had a tough past, but you've got a lot to look forward to."

Carter raised an eyebrow. "And how's that working out for you?"

Blake's face softened. "Ever since I met Tara, I've had bigger things to think about—like potty training the twins."

Carter's eyes widened. "Sounds terrifying."

"It is!" Blake said, looking horrified. "Dad life. But it's amazing. It gives everything a different perspective."

Carter left the restaurant, Blake's words swirling around his head like a storm he couldn't escape. Was he right? Were there other things in life than adrenaline? The afternoon sun had faded into a dim glow behind the clouds, casting a muted light over the city streets.

His phone vibrated, and he glanced down to see a text from Eleanor: *I set up a meeting tomorrow with Grant Technologies. It's looking really good.*

He frowned, typing back quickly. *We're not moving forward with David. He's a liability.*

He hit send and immediately tried calling her, but it went straight to voicemail. "Damn it, Eleanor," he muttered, slipping his phone back into his pocket.

CHAPTER 11

Sophia's phone chimed with a last-minute meeting invite from Eleanor set for first thing in the morning. That was surprising. As she glanced at the details, she brushed back her long dark hair, her blue eyes narrowing with suspicion as her mind wandered to yesterday's lunch with Carter.

She got to the office early and decided to stop at the coffee shop next door. But as soon as she walked in, she spotted Carter already in line. *Great.*

He waved her over, tall and muscular, flashing that easy, charming smile. "Morning. *Join me?*"

Sophia hesitated but moved to stand next to him. The barista, clearly flustered by Carter's presence, was practically falling over herself with smiles and compliments. Carter was polite, his attention on Sophia.

"And whatever she's having," he said, nodding at Sophia.

"Thanks, but you didn't have to do that," she said, feeling a bit awkward.

Carter shrugged. "Just being a gentleman. Besides, I still owe you after you ditched that salad yesterday." He grinned.

She laughed, genuinely amused. "I guess I didn't really eat, did I?"

"Nope," he said, handing her the coffee. "You were too busy giving me the third degree before making your grand escape."

She took the cup, feeling a warm, tingly sensation spread

through her that had nothing to do with the coffee. His eyes were on her, that playful, almost too-intense gaze making it hard to remember why she was supposed to keep her guard up. "I didn't give you the third degree," she insisted, trying to ignore the way his smile was doing things to her body.

"Oh, right," he teased, leaning in just enough that she could catch a hint of his cologne. "So, grilling me on my favorite wine *wasn't* the third degree?"

She tried to look annoyed, but a smile slipped through. "That wasn't grilling. That was *small* talk."

He tilted his head, a slow, playful grin spreading across his face. "If that's your idea of *small* talk, I'm almost afraid to see what you do on a date."

She cleared her throat, trying to ignore what he'd just said. *Did he just mention a date? With her?* No, focus. He was just teasing. "Well, let's just say my interrogation skills are top-notch. Comes in handy when I'm moonlighting for the FBI," she joked, raising an eyebrow.

She tried to steer the conversation back to safe ground, but her mind kept circling back. *Was that a hint?* No, of course not. This was business, and he was *definitely* not supposed to be getting to her like this. But the way he was looking at her...

As they walked out, she caught a whiff of his cologne—or maybe it was his aftershave. Whatever it was, it smelled incredible. His tall, muscular frame seemed to close the space between them, and being this close to him was starting to mess with her head.

They made their way to the elevator, chatting easily. But once inside, a crowd of people quickly filled the space, and they were pressed up against each other, his shoulder brushing hers. The slight contact sent a jolt of electricity through her body.

Carter glanced down at her, clearly aware of the sudden

closeness. "Comfortable?" he joked softly, his breath warm against her ear.

Her pulse raced. No, this was not good. She couldn't be responding to him like this—her body betraying her mind's resolve. "Very," she managed, the word catching as she fought to keep her composure.

The elevator jolted as it started to move, pressing him even closer against her. His scent enveloped her, and she forced herself to focus on the floor numbers lighting up above them, silently willing the ride to be over before she did something embarrassing, like lean into him.

Finally, the elevator doors slid open, and they stepped out together. They walked side by side to the meeting room, their steps falling into an easy rhythm. She caught herself almost smiling—almost—as they reached the door.

But as soon as they entered, Eleanor swooped in, all business and edges. "Carter, I need a quick word," she said, her eyes darting between them.

"Of course," he replied, casting a brief glance at Sophia before following Eleanor across the room.

From her seat, Sophia watched as they disappeared into a smaller conference room. Through the glass walls, she could see Carter and Eleanor talking—no, arguing. Carter's face was tense, his gestures controlled, while Eleanor's expression was a mix of frustration and determination.

Then, the door to the main conference room opened, and her brother, David, strolled in with a smug grin. *What the hell?* Sophia's heart pounded. David hadn't set foot in Grant Technologies in years. What was he doing here now?

She watched as he moved around the room, greeting a few familiar faces, his presence as cocky as ever. Something was definitely off. Carter and Eleanor's argument seemed to be escalating, and she noticed the way Carter's expression darkened when he glanced in David's direction.

Moments later, Carter walked into the main room, his gaze sweeping over the assembled staff. He looked frustrated, almost... angry?

"There's been a misunderstanding," he announced, his voice firm but strained. "This meeting is canceled."

A ripple of confusion passed through the room as people exchanged bewildered glances.

"I apologize for the confusion," Carter continued, his tone intense. "But everyone can get back to work."

The tension was palpable as he stepped back, his eyes flicking briefly to Sophia before he turned away. David, visibly furious, stormed out in the direction Eleanor had gone, his face set in a scowl.

Sophia was left reeling, completely lost. What was David doing here? And what was going on? She headed to the bathroom, her thoughts a tangled mess. Standing in front of the mirror, she took out her lipstick, mechanically reapplying it while trying to piece everything together.

Why was David there? Her lawyer had said he was buying up shares, but what did that even mean? Had David come back just to make her life hell?

She took a deep breath, staring at her reflection. *Get it together, Sophia.* Whatever this was, she needed to be ready.

Steeling herself, she pushed open the bathroom door and stepped out—only to find Eleanor standing there, arms crossed, as if she'd been waiting.

"Eleanor," Sophia said, her voice biting than she intended. "What the hell is going on?"

Eleanor's expression was guarded, but there was something flickering in her eyes—nervousness? "We need to talk," she said quietly, glancing around to make sure they were alone.

"What do you want?" Sophia asked, trying to keep her voice consistent despite the whirlwind inside her.

Eleanor's smirk deepened as she reached into her leather bag, pulling out a crisp, folded document. Without a word, she extended it toward Sophia.

Sophia glanced at it, then back at Eleanor. "What is this?"

"Oh, I think you'll want to read it," Eleanor purred, her voice dripping with false sweetness.

Sophia hesitated, her fingers brushing over the edge of the crisp folder Eleanor had shoved into her hands. Something felt off—this wasn't just another business maneuver. The look on Eleanor's face was too pleased, too certain of her power in this moment.

With a deep breath, Sophia flipped open the folder. Her heart plummeted as her eyes scanned the text, the words blurring together for a moment before snapping into clarity.

A **pre-signed takeover agreement**.

Her board—her trusted allies—had signed it. Each signature was neatly aligned, confirming that the sale of Grant Technologies to Carter Kane was all but finalized. Her breath hitched, panic rising as her stomach twisted.

"They've already signed?" Sophia's voice was hoarse, barely more than a whisper, her hand trembling as she clutched the document. She couldn't believe what she was reading. "But they can't—I'm the CEO."

"Not anymore," Eleanor replied coolly, her eyes hard. "David's in charge now."

"That's impossible," Sophia said, her voice shaking. "He can't just take over."

Eleanor's smile was almost pitiful. "He has majority shares now. The board signed this morning. It's done. Bye-bye, Sophia."

Sophia's stomach churned, a wave of nausea hitting her hard. How could this be happening? Hadn't she been careful? Was David really willing to go this far?

Her mind reeled, and a new, sharper pain stabbed through her. *Did Carter know about this?* He'd bought her coffee this morning, acted friendly, like they were on the same side. And now, this?

"That bastard," she whispered, more to herself than to Eleanor. "He played me. He acted like my best friend and then stabbed me in the back."

Eleanor shrugged, looking almost bored. "It's just business, Sophia. Some people are better at playing the game."

Sophia needed answers—and fast. She was beyond angry, a boiling rage simmering under the surface. Was this really happening? She dialed her attorney, her hands shaking, but the call went straight to voicemail. "Joshua, call me back. *Now.*" She hung up, her heart pounding. Did he know about this? Was *everyone* in on it?

Her mind spun, the pieces snapping into place. David had been quietly buying shares to push her out. That snake. She'd spent years begging him to get involved, to join the family business. But no—he was too busy doing who-knows-what while she burned the midnight oil with their dad, learning every facet of the company. And when he finally decided to grace them with his presence, he bailed after a month! Now he's trying to push her out? Unbelievable.

She clutched her phone, fury mixing with the sting of betrayal. Why would he do this? She would have welcomed him back if he'd shown the slightest interest. But no—he'd swooped in when it suited him, with no idea how much blood, sweat, and tears she'd poured into this place.

Desperate for answers, she dialed Richard from the board—someone she was sure had been on her side. The call went straight to voicemail. Her heart sank as she listened to his automated message, each beep feeling like another betrayal. She hung up, frustration boiling over, and quickly dialed her mom's number instead.

"Mom, it's me..." she said, her voice breaking as soon as the line connected. She didn't wait for a greeting. "Why would David do it? Why would he steal the company out from under me? I don't understand!" The sobs she'd been holding back finally escaped, and she felt her mother's soft, worried voice try to soothe her through the phone, but it only made the hurt more unbearable.

There was a pause, and then her mom's voice came through, confused. "What do you mean? David wouldn't do that."

"Mom, he already did!" Sophia cried, her voice trembling. "He's taken control. He's ousted me. The board voted me out. I'm not CEO anymore."

Her mom sounded shaken. "But... your father built that company. Why would David want it? He was never interested."

"Exactly!" Sophia snapped, swiping angrily at the tears streaming down her face. "He never cared. And now, out of nowhere, he's buying shares like he's been planning this for years. Dad would be furious."

There was a long silence before her mom spoke again, her voice low and pained. "David's been in a bit of trouble lately, sweetheart. I didn't want to worry you, but... I'm sure he wouldn't do anything to hurt you or the company."

Sophia's heart sank. "It's too late for that, Mom," she whispered. "He already has. I've got to go. I have to put on a happy face for this charity event tonight, and I need to meet with a lawyer—quickly."

"Okay, sweetheart," her mom said softly, but there was a lingering sadness in her voice. "I'm so sorry, Sophia. I wish I could do something."

"I know, Mom," she said, her voice breaking. "I'll call you later."

She hung up and took a shaky breath, her thoughts spinning. Then she pulled out her phone and stared at Evan's text. Her first instinct was to ignore it—diving back into that mess was the last thing she needed. But right now, she needed answers, and Evan was a good attorney. Maybe he could help her navigate this nightmare with David.

Sorry, been busy. But lunch sounds good. Can you do today? she typed, then hit send. She didn't want to reopen old wounds, but if anyone could help her make sense of this legal mess, it was him.

CHAPTER 12

Carter was furious. He barely managed to keep his voice steady as he leaned over his desk, his eyes locked on Eleanor. "You called a meeting without telling me, made a move without my knowledge. We agreed—no decisions without me."

Eleanor's eyes narrowed, but her smile didn't falter. "You weren't moving fast enough. We've waited long enough. I did what needed to be done."

"What needed to be done?" He stood, towering over the desk. "You made a move without consulting me? Without even telling me? It's been, what, two weeks? That's not exactly dragging your feet, Eleanor."

"Everything's here," she said, her voice triumphant as she tossed a folder onto his desk. "It's done, Carter. We have everything we need."

His eyes flicked to the folder, the Grant Technologies logo emblazoned on the front. "What are you talking about?"

"This," she said, gesturing to the folder with a smug smile. "Signatures from every single board member. The takeover is officially complete."

He stared at the folder, the bold black ink blurring as he processed her words. Disbelief surged through him, quickly replaced by a burning, visceral anger. "You went behind my back?" His voice was low, dangerous.

"David isn't the right guy for CEO. He doesn't know the company, he's unstable—"

"It doesn't matter," she cut in, her tone dismissive. "The board's on our side. We've got the shares. It's too late for second thoughts now."

"It's not too late to get this *right*," he growled, slamming his palm down on the desk. "I brought you into this because you said you wanted to be a part of it, but I'm the one in charge, and we need to be strategic. David will run this company into the ground— I've dealt with enough guys like him to know. Stop undermining me. Sophia is the one who can keep things running smoothly."

Eleanor's eyes flashed with irritation. "She's out, Carter. It's over. David's in control, and there's nothing you can do about it."

"Do you have some personal vendetta against Sophia? Do you not like her?" Carter's voice was crisp, his frustration boiling over.

"Yes, Carter," Eleanor snapped, her eyes blazing. "That's the whole point. This is about revenge. Remember?" She paused, her voice dropping, the anger replaced by something raw and broken.

"You weren't there, Carter. You didn't see him afterward. The man who used to command a room couldn't even look at himself in the mirror. I found him that night... with a bottle of pills in his hand. He was ready to give up—on everything. I'm pushing so hard because *you* convinced me it was the Grants' fault. You're the one who said they ruined him. And I won't let you or anyone else make me feel guilty for fighting back."

"But the Grants didn't put that pill bottle in his hand," Carter shot back. "Sophia didn't do this to him. She didn't give him Alzheimer's."

Eleanor's face twisted with a mix of anger and pain. "Are you serious? You were the one who told me that the stress and humiliation from their betrayal pushed him over the edge. And now you're saying it's not their fault?"

Carter shook his head, frustration simmering beneath the surface. "It's not that simple, Eleanor. It could have been anything—genetics, life—sometimes things just happen, and it's not always someone's fault."

"You're the one who convinced me!" Eleanor's voice cracked. "You wanted this. You made me believe we needed to take Grant Technologies down. So why did you do that, Carter?"

He hesitated, memories flooding back.

"He told me it was James Grant's fault—that everything that happened to him, his downfall, was because of James."

Eleanor's eyes narrowed. "When did he say that, Carter? Before or after he lost his memory? Because he's said a lot of things that don't make sense." She shook her head, frustration and pain mixing in her expression. "He thinks he's living in the '70s half the time. Last week, he asked me if I'd fed the dog. We never *had* a dog."

The reality of it hit. *He* was the one who had started this whole damn mess, feeding Eleanor the idea that it was some kind of justice.

"I'm sorry," he said softly, looking at her with genuine regret. "I didn't mean for it to get this far."

Eleanor looked away, her anger simmering. "Well, it has. And now, thanks to you, we're both in too deep."

His gut twisted with guilt. This wasn't victory. Maybe he had it all wrong. He'd taken down his so-called rival, and instead of feeling triumphant, he felt hollow. Sophia hadn't done anything wrong, other than being in the wrong place at the wrong time. And now, she was paying for it.

He'd never felt this way before—remorse? A conscience, like Blake had put it. It stung, and he hated that it was so new, so foreign.

And now Eleanor had gone behind his back and forced Sophia out, just like that. He could be angry at Eleanor, but deep down, he knew he was the one to blame. He'd been ruthless, he'd been the one who didn't care about collateral damage. And now, crap, this wasn't winning. This was just losing, in a different way.

Eleanor looked at him, her expression a mix of sadness and irritation, before turning and leaving the office in silence. He watched her go, the documents she'd slammed down still sitting on his desk like a lead weight.

As he flipped through the documents, something caught his eye. A small, technical error in one of the clauses—a loophole that could potentially void the entire agreement. It was a small mistake, easily missed, but it was there.

A lifeline.

He sank back, staring at the papers in his hand. This was his chance to undo it all. To give Sophia a fighting chance, even if it meant losing everything he'd fought for.

The realization smacked him in the face: Was he actually considering sabotaging his own takeover? No, no, no. Sure, he took over companies—sometimes ruthlessly—but he was always upfront about it. He didn't do business like this. Not sneaky, and certainly not underhanded.

His phone vibrated on the desk, breaking the silence. He glanced at the screen—Blake. For a moment, he considered ignoring it, but then he picked up.

"Hey, man," Blake's voice came through, easy and familiar. "Just checking in. You want to grab a beer?"

"Sure," he said finally. "I could use a drink."

Carter dropped his phone onto the desk, glancing at the folder Eleanor had left. He didn't want to look, but he couldn't avoid it.

He exhaled slowly, leaning back in his chair. The folder lay open, the documents inside taunting him with their finality.

His eyes skimmed the signatures of board members who, with a few pen strokes, had handed Sophia's company over to David. People she likely trusted, now selling her out in a heartbeat. It didn't sit right.

One call, and I could fix this. Or I could let it all burn.

His phone rang again, a brief flash of Blake's name on the screen. Right. They were supposed to meet. He needed to get out of here, away from this office, away from Eleanor's manipulations, away from the pressure closing in on him from all sides.

Grabbing his jacket, he took one last look at the closed drawer. The error in the agreement felt like a ticking clock, counting down to a moment that would change everything. He had to decide what mattered more—winning or doing what was right.

He arrived at the restaurant, grateful for the dim lighting and the relative quiet. Blake was already there, a beer in hand, watching him with a knowing look.

"Rough day?" Blake asked, his tone light but his eyes focused.

Carter slid into the seat opposite him, nodding slowly. "You could say that."

Blake took a sip of his drink, waiting. When Carter didn't speak, he leaned forward. "Want to talk about it?"

For a moment, Carter hesitated. Then, in a rush, he told Blake everything—about the mistake in the documents, about Eleanor's betrayal, about undoing what Eleanor had done. That he was grateful that Sophia didn't know yet.

Blake listened, his expression thoughtful. When Carter finally fell silent, Blake shook his head slowly. "Sounds like you're in deep, man. This isn't just about the company anymore, is it?"

Carter laughed bitterly. "I wish it were that simple."

"Look," Blake said, leaning forward, his voice serious. "I've known you a long time. You're a good guy. But you've been so focused on this revenge thing, I think you've lost sight of what's really important. If undoing this feels right, then do it. But don't do it halfway. If you're gonna play the hero, go all in or go home."

Carter stared at him, the words sinking in slowly. Be the good guy. It sounded so simple, but it felt like the hardest thing in the world. "It's not that easy," he muttered. "I don't know if I can just... let it go."

Blake shrugged. "Maybe you can't. But maybe you can do something else. You don't have to destroy her to win, Carter. Maybe winning means something different now."

They finished their beers, the conversation drifting to safer topics, but Carter's mind kept circling back to Sophia.

Then he spotted her, just a few feet away, sitting with another man at a booth. Her posture was tense, her expression serious. Carter's chest tightened painfully.

Blake followed his eyes. "You know her?"

"Yeah. I know her."

He couldn't tear his eyes away as Sophia edged forward, her fingers brushing the man's arm in a way that felt too close, too intimate. Jealousy hit him, something unfamiliar.

Blake watched him, concerned. "You okay, man?"

Carter forced himself to look away, nodding stiffly. "Yeah. I'm fine."

But he wasn't fine. Seeing her there, with someone else, flipped a switch inside him. Why was he so hell-bent on protecting her? This was getting personal, and he could feel himself teetering—he could help her, or he could crush her.

As he headed toward the exit, something made him glance back, and he locked eyes with Sophia. Her expression shifted— she looked genuinely sad, a flash of betrayal in her eyes. Before he knew it, he was awkwardly stopping by their table, feeling compelled to say something, anything.

The man with her looked up, his gaze flicking between them. Sophia's eyes stayed on Carter, a mix of hurt and anger in her expression.

Carter's throat tightened. For once, he was at a loss for words. He just nodded, feeling like an idiot, and left the restaurant, her haunted look burned into his mind. *Why did she look at him like that?* She didn't know Eleanor had tried to replace her as CEO. He'd canceled *that* meeting before Sophia found out, and he would fix this before she did.

CHAPTER 13

Sophia leaned against the sink in the bathroom, trying to collect herself. Why did Carter have to be everywhere she went? And that look he gave her—like a lost puppy dog. It was infuriating.

She took a deep breath, glancing at her reflection. She needed to get back to lunch with Evan. She wasn't interested in reconnecting with him personally, but he was a lawyer, and her own attorney wasn't returning her calls. Evan wasn't exactly a corporate lawyer—more of a divorce specialist—but right now, she'd take whatever help she could get.

She had barely been there five minutes before Carter showed up and rattled her. With one last deep breath, she straightened and stepped out of the bathroom, forcing a calm expression as she approached their table.

Evan looked up, concern etched on his face. "You okay?"

"Fine," she said with a forced smile. "Just had to use the restroom."

"So, that was the guy doing this to you?" Evan asked as she sat down.

"Yeah," Sophia replied, her smile strained. "The one trying to take over my company."

Evan paused, looking genuinely surprised. "I'm sorry, Sophia. Do you have the paperwork? You know I'm not a corporate lawyer, right?"

"I know," she sighed, pulling out the documents. "But I need someone to look at this, and my own lawyer isn't calling me back." She hesitated, then continued, "That reminds me, my brother David is the one who somehow orchestrated all of this. You remember David. Can you believe it? He never had any interest in the company, and now this?"

Evan's expression shifted, his eyes darting away. He looked... awkward.

"What's up?" Sophia asked, her voice cool.

He cleared his throat. "I thought you knew. I took on David's divorce case after Becky left."

Sophia's jaw dropped. "What? You're representing him?"

"Yeah," Evan said, looking uncomfortable. "David knew I was a divorce lawyer and reached out when everything fell apart with Becky."

"Oh my God," Sophia muttered, leaning back in her chair. "Tell me everything. Does it make sense why he'd do this?"

Evan shook his head quickly. "Sophia, I can't break client privilege. But... I'm not surprised."

She pressed forward, her voice urgent. "Please, Evan. I need to understand why he's doing this."

"I really can't discuss it, Sophia," he said, his tone firm but apologetic.

She frowned, feeling the frustration building. "Can you at least review the documents? See if there's something I'm missing?"

Evan sighed, glancing at the papers. "It might present a conflict of interest, considering I'm working with David. I think it's best if we change the topic."

Sophia stared at him, disbelief and rage churning inside her. "Are you serious? That's literally why I'm here. I need help, and you're going to side with my brother and keep quiet?"

He looked genuinely pained. "I have no choice, Sophia. I'm sorry."

"I thought the divorce was final," she said, frustration creeping into her voice.

Evan shook his head. "I really can't talk about it."

Her frustration spiked. Why had she even called him? They broke up because of his endless lies, and now, here she was, hoping for honesty. Even if he did tell her something, could she even trust it?

"This was a mistake," she muttered, pushing her plate away.

Evan looked down, then back up at her with a hint of exasperation. "It's always about work with you. *Work work work.* Yes, this was a mistake."

She scoffed. "And yours was lying, remember?" She stood up, grabbing her bag. "I need to call my *actual* lawyer. And get ready for a charity event tonight."

Evan nodded, looking like he wanted to say more but held back. She stood up, grateful the awkward lunch was over. She paid the bill quickly, muttered a stiff goodbye, and left, not looking back as she made her way to the door.

Outside, she took a deep breath, the cold air hitting her face. At least now she could focus on what mattered—getting her company back.

Sophia left the restaurant and got into her car, slamming the door shut with a frustrated sigh. She considered calling Jessica, her COO and friend—or at least she had thought so—but then remembered how oddly distant she'd been lately. Pulling out the stack of documents, she scanned them quickly, her eyes freezing on Jessica's signature, bold and unmistakable among the others.

Her stomach dropped. Jessica, too? Betrayal hit her like a punch. Another person she'd trusted, gone.

Her phone buzzed, and she saw her lawyer's name flash on the screen. *Finally.* "I've been tied up all day," he said quickly.

"Did you hear what happened?" she asked, her voice tight.

"Their legal counsel notified me, but I haven't had a chance to go through the paperwork yet," he admitted.

"Can we meet early tomorrow?" she pressed. "I have an event tonight, but I need to sort this out as soon as possible."

He agreed, and she hung up, the conversation doing little to ease her anxiety. She drove home. Somehow, she had to hold it together for this charity event, to smile and act like her world wasn't crumbling around her. She took a deep breath, steeling herself. Tonight, she'd show up with her head held high.

CHAPTER 14

Carter needed to focus. Eleanor and David's plans were spread out in front of him like a chessboard, but all he could see was Sophia with Evan, their heads bent close. He knew exactly who Evan was—a high-profile divorce attorney. Why was she talking to him? But what really got to him was the look she'd given Carter, like he'd killed her dog and told her Santa Claus wasn't real. Brutal.

The door swung open, and, as if on cue, Eleanor strode in, her expression a mask of confidence. Perfect timing.

"You need to undo this, Eleanor," Carter said, his voice tight. "We don't know anything about David, other than he's trying to get control of a company we're supposed to be taking over."

Eleanor raised an eyebrow. "Grant Technologies wasn't a done deal, Carter. Now, with David as CEO, it is. He has the majority and controls the board. We get Sophia out, and we control David. He'll do what we say, no questions asked."

"This is a terrible plan," Carter shot back, stepping around his desk. "Why the hell did you go behind my back?"

Eleanor shrugged, completely unbothered. "I was taking care of business. You should be thanking me."

"Thanking you?" Carter's voice was low, simmering with bitterness. "It's not done yet. You might have the paperwork, but you're not going to do *anything* with it."

Eleanor's smile was smug, almost condescending. "I already gave it to Sophia. It's a done deal."

Carter's blood ran cold. "What?" Everything clicked into place—the look Sophia had given him, like he was the one holding the knife. "You had no right to execute without telling me, Eleanor."

"Stop being so dramatic, Carter," she huffed, glancing at her watch. "I have to go try on dresses. This is handled."

"Handled?" He stared at her, disbelief mingling with fury. "Well, consider it *unhandled*."

Eleanor let out a short, derisive laugh. "Please, Carter. Maybe you need to blow off some steam and stop pretending you have a conscience." She crossed her arms. "I have more important things to deal with right now—I have a wedding to plan, a dress to find, and someone who actually loves me."

"Eleanor—"

"We *need* this deal to go through, Carter. *I need this.*" She cut him off sharply. " To pay for the wedding, among other things. And since you don't have to worry about money, stop messing with mine." With that, she spun on her heel and stormed out, leaving him seething, staring at the empty doorway.

Oh, so this was about money. Is that why she wanted in on this deal so badly? He could just give her the damn cash if that was the issue—but not when she was acting like a dramatic teenager. And he didn't do business like this. Sure, he was ruthless, but not underhanded. Eleanor had crossed a line.

Yes, he'd played his part, but he didn't work behind people's backs. Eleanor's underhanded tactics infuriated him more than he cared to admit. He hadn't built his empire on shady deals, and he wasn't about to start now. Decision made—he'd find Sophia and set the record straight.

But where the hell was she? Then he remembered—the charity event. She'd mentioned it at least five times, and she'd even emailed the whole office about it yesterday. *She sure was thorough!*

Great. Looked like he was going to a charity event.

He left the office, heading home to change into something more appropriate. If he was going to show up, he wasn't about to look like a schmuck—especially not when he needed to apologize. An apology was going to be hard enough without looking like he'd just come from a boardroom brawl. He'd have to get this right.

Carter pulled up to the hotel, handing his keys to the valet as he glanced around. He tried to remember what tonight's event was for—childhood cancer, maybe? He vaguely recalled that Sophia was on the board for something like that. Whatever it was, she was deeply involved.

He straightened his tie and handed his invitation to the doorman. Taking a breath, he walked inside. The grand ballroom was alive with the city's elite, their laughter mingling with the soft notes of a string quartet. Crystal chandeliers bathed everything in a golden glow, but he barely noticed—he was focused on finding her.

And then he saw her.

Sophia stood across the room, her back to him, speaking with a group of donors. The emerald dress she wore clung to her curves, elegant and understated, and his breath caught. But it wasn't just her beauty that drew him. It was the way she held herself—straight and poised, her chin lifted as if she were daring anyone to see her falter. Her smile was in place, but her eyes... they told a different story.

His frustration with Eleanor, his jealousy over Evan—it all seemed petty now. What mattered was fixing this, showing her that he didn't do business like that.

He was going to make things right.

Carter wove through the crowd, eyes locked on Sophia. His heart pounded as he brushed off greetings and dodged small talk, barely noticing the laughter and music around him. When she spotted him, surprise flickered across her face before it hardened into wary caution.

Then the lights dimmed, and a hush fell over the crowd as the announcer urged everyone to take their seats. Carter watched as Sophia moved to a table a few rows away, her back straight, her attention seemingly focused elsewhere.

He sighed and found a seat, cursing his luck. Damn it, he hated these events—people pretending to care about causes they barely understood. He'd play along, eat dinner, nod at the right moments, and then make his move as soon as the speeches were done.

The first speaker stepped up to the mic, launching into the usual script. Thank you all for being here, supporting this important cause. Then all he heard was *blah blah blah*. Carter tuned it out as he picked at his dinner.

But then the speaker's tone shifted, pulling him in. "If you know someone going through this, I understand how personal it is for you. Watching a loved one struggle with dementia or Alzheimer's is heartbreaking. It's more than just memory loss —it's watching someone you love slip away. The confusion, the frustration, the moments when they don't recognize you... it's devastating."

Carter froze, his fork halfway to his mouth. *This is for Alzheimer's?*

The speaker continued, describing the slow, painful decline, the helplessness of being unable to do anything to stop it.

The speaker stepped aside, and a woman took the stage, her smile warm but tinged with sadness.

"Good evening," she began, her voice emotional. "I'm here tonight to share a story about my father, Michael. He was the kind of man who never forgot a birthday, who could recite every baseball stat from memory, and who always remembered to tell me I was his favorite girl."

She paused, her eyes scanning the room. "A few years ago, he started forgetting things—small things at first. He would misplace his keys or forget what day it was. We laughed it off, thinking it was just part of getting older. But then he started getting confused about who I was. He'd call me by my mother's name, even though she'd been gone for years."

Her voice wavered slightly, but she pressed on. "The day I knew something was really wrong was when he didn't recognize me at all. I walked into his room, and he looked at me like I was a stranger. I remember him asking, 'Who are you, young lady?' And I—I didn't know how to answer."

She took a deep breath, holding back tears. "Watching him disappear was the hardest thing I've ever been through. It's like losing someone you love a thousand times. You lose their laugh, their stories, their way of remembering all the little things about you that no one else does. And the worst part is, they know it's happening too. They're scared and angry, and there's nothing you can do to make it stop."

The room was utterly silent, everyone captivated by her words.

"That's why I'm here tonight—to support the research, the care, and the hope that someday, families like mine won't have to go through this. Because no one should have to watch the person they love fade away, helpless to do anything but watch."

She took a step back, her voice steadier now. "Thank you all for being here and for helping us fight this disease. For giving us hope that one day, we'll find a cure."

The audience erupted into applause, and Carter felt something tighten in his chest. He glanced at Sophia, who was watching the stage intently, and for the first time, he realized this event was more than just another charity appearance for her.

Carter struggled to keep it together. He'd never talked about watching his dad fade away, never thought about others going through the same thing. For a moment, he felt less alone. But being here, reminded of his father's decline, hurt more than he expected. Rivalries and revenue felt meaningless amidst the quiet grief of those who had also watched someone they loved disappear.

The event wrapped up, and he wiped at his eyes, trying to clear away the emotion that had surfaced. It was too much. He felt raw, exposed. As he made his way out, he decided he needed to do something, anything. He stopped by the donation table and scribbled a generous amount, hoping it would ease some of the guilt gnawing at him.

Sophia was across the room, heading for the door. He moved quickly, catching her just as she reached the exit.

"Sophia," he called out, his voice still thick with emotion. She turned, her eyes widening in surprise as he approached.

She narrowed her eyes, her voice low and tense. "This isn't the time, Carter."

"It's important. Please."

She hesitated, her fingers tightening around the stem of her glass. Then, with a sigh, she set it down on the nearest table and turned to the small group she'd been talking to, offering them a polite, "Excuse me for a moment." She glanced back at Carter, her expression unreadable. "Fine. Let's talk."

He guided her to a quieter corner of the room, away from the curious stares and raised eyebrows. As soon as they were out of earshot, she crossed her arms, her posture defensive, and he hated that she looked at him like that, like he was someone she couldn't trust. But he didn't blame her. Not after what Eleanor had done.

"Sophia," he began, his voice firm but gentle. "I know Eleanor gave you the takeover documents. I swear, I didn't know she was going to do that. I never would have blindsided you like that."

A flicker of hurt crossed her face. "What do you want me to say, Carter? That I believe you?"

"I had no part in this mess. I didn't want to corner you. I wanted a clean fight. To win it straight up—not like this." He had a feeling that everything had gone wrong. "I don't do business like this."

She looked away. "What difference does it make? It's done, isn't it? You got what you wanted."

"No," he said quickly, stepping closer. "Not like this. I didn't want this. I would never have gone behind your back, never would have let Eleanor pull something like this if I'd known."

She searched his face, as if looking for some sign that he was telling the truth. "You really didn't know?"

"No," he said softly, sincerity in every word. "But I may have found a clause buried in the paperwork that could help you out."

For a moment, she just stared at him, then shook her head slowly. "I don't know what to think anymore, Carter. I don't know who to trust."

The vulnerability in her voice twisted something deep inside him. He reached out, hesitating for just a second before gently touching her arm. "Trust me. Please. We're on the same side, Sophia. Or at least, we *should* be."

She studied him, her eyes searching his. Then, slowly, she nodded. "Okay."

Relief washed over him, and he let out a breath he hadn't realized he was holding.

They settled into chairs at the back, away from the noise and prying eyes. He waved down a waiter for drinks to ease the tension. They spoke carefully.

As they talked, the tension between them softened. They weren't opponents here, not anymore. Here, tonight... he was just a man.

More drinks arrived, and the conversation loosened up. He definitely needed something to wash down the emotions from that unexpected presentation. Whatever her connection to the event, he wasn't ready to swap sob stories. Instead, they traded tales of their early days in business. Against his better judgment, he found himself leaning in, hooked on every word, mesmerized by the fire in her voice. Damn. When did this turn into the most interesting meeting of his day?

Then, in a quiet moment between topics, he shifted the conversation, his voice lighter. "I saw somewhere that you like to run. I can't imagine you finding the time with your schedule."

She laughed softly, a real laugh that made his heart skip. "I used to run to clear my head, but now I'm lucky if I hit the gym once a month. You seem more like a 'take out your stress on a punching bag' kind of person."

He chuckled, shaking his head. "I tried running for a while. Got up at five every morning for a few months, convinced myself I'd found the secret to success."

"And?" She raised an eyebrow, a playful challenge in her eyes.

"I hated it. Seriously, running is just organized torture. Breathing and moving at the same time? Total nightmare."

She laughed again, and he felt a rush of warmth at the sound. "Tell me about it. I thought it would be relaxing, but I spent the whole time mentally cursing every step."

"Same here." He shifted back, his expression softening as he looked at her. "I finally gave it up when I realized I was more stressed about my running goals than anything else."

Her smile turned wistful. "I guess we both gave up then. I thought I could run away from all the pressure, but I ended up just running in circles."

There was a moment of silence, something unspoken passing between them. He wanted to reach out, to tell her that he understood, that he knew what it felt like to carry expectations, of always feeling like you had to prove yourself. But he held back, not wanting to push too far too fast.

Another round of drinks arrived, and they continued talking, their conversation shifting from business to personal anecdotes, to dreams and regrets. The walls between them, so carefully constructed over time, were beginning to crumble, brick by brick.

Carter was captivated by the way her eyes lit up as she talked about her father's company and her vision for its future. She was brilliant, determined, and stronger than anyone realized. The more she spoke, the more he was drawn to her—almost forgetting she was James Grant's daughter. Did that even matter anymore? He was getting himself into trouble, and he knew it.

"Ever think about what you'd do if you weren't in this corporate grind?"

"Honestly?" He shrugged, a wry smile forming. "I've thought about getting out on the water. Not those big yachts, though. I like the smaller boats—something I can take out alone, where I can get some peace."

She laughed, the sound soft and melodic. "You? On a tiny boat? I can't picture it."

"Why not?" he teased. "I'm pretty good with a sail. It's the downtime I'd struggle with. I'd probably end up turning the whole thing into a charter business within a month."

"I knew it," she said, her eyes sparkling. "You can't switch off. You're too driven."

"Maybe." He looked at her, his expression turning serious. "But I'm trying. And right now, I'm trying to be here. To fix this."

She stared down at her glass, tracing the rim with her finger. "I don't know, Carter. I've worked my whole life for this career, and now I'm starting to wonder if it's even worth it anymore."

"I get it," he said quietly. "I've felt the same way. You give everything, and then suddenly you're questioning if it's all been for nothing."

The drinks kept coming, and the atmosphere between them softened. His male instincts were definitely kicking in, and he couldn't ignore how her glance lingered on him a little longer. Any warning signals about this being dangerous territory were quickly dismissed. He just knew he didn't want the night to end.

He swayed forward, his voice low and tentative. "Come back to my place. We can talk. No more business—just talk."

She hesitated, her eyes holding his with a look that said *oh, sure…just talk.* The air between them felt charged and unspoken. For a second, he thought she'd laugh and shut him down, retreating back behind those walls—but she didn't.

But then, slowly, she nodded. "Okay."

CHAPTER 15

Sophia stared out the Uber window as city lights blurred past. She couldn't believe she was here, next to Carter, heading to his place. Her mind spun, replaying the night's events on a loop..

She hadn't expected to see him at the event, let alone hear him apologize. But there he was, saying he hadn't known about Eleanor's plan, that this wasn't how he did business. And what shocked her most was that she believed him—at least, she thought she did. There was something sincere in his eyes that had completely thrown her off.

Her heart fluttered as she glanced at him. He stared straight ahead, his profile serious in the dim light. Why had she agreed to go back to his place after everything? It felt surreal, like she was watching herself make one questionable choice after another. But the wine was like a little devil on her shoulder, urging her to let loose and forget about work for once.

What am I doing? The thought echoed in her mind, mixing doubt with the warmth of his words. She knew she should be cautious, not drop her guard over a few kind gestures. But it was hard to keep her defenses up when he looked at her like that, with that rough, quiet intensity that made her want to believe him.

Betrayed by Eleanor, her brother, Jessica, Evan, and even her own company—the last person she expected to lean on was Carter. He was supposed to be the enemy.

Yet here she was, sitting next to him, emotions twisted into something she hadn't anticipated.

And that thought shook her. If he wasn't trying to force her out and actually wanted to work with her, then what did that mean for them? For her?

She settled back against the seat, closing her eyes for a moment. It felt good to let go, to stop fighting, even if it was just for *one night*. It was ironic, really—here she was, letting her guard down around the very person who'd been the source of so much of her stress. But she couldn't deny that it was a relief to just be *Sophia*, not the CEO, not James Grant's daughter, just herself.

Carter shifted beside her, and she opened her eyes, catching a glimpse of him glancing at her from the corner of his eye. There was a tension in his posture, a kind of focused intensity that sent a thrill through her, despite everything. What was he thinking? Was he as conflicted as she was, or did he have everything neatly compartmentalized, like he always seemed to?

What in the hell am I doing? She wondered again, but the question felt less urgent now, less desperate. Because despite the chaos of the past few weeks, despite everything that had gone wrong, she was here, and she was... happy? No, not happy. But something close. Relaxed, maybe. Relieved. And for the first time in what felt like forever, she wasn't bracing for the next blow, the next piece of bad news.

As the Uber turned onto a private drive, the house came into view. Her breath caught. She knew Carter was wealthy, but this was next level. The estate was a stunning blend of refined lines and glass, framed by manicured gardens. Lights bathed the modern masterpiece in a warm glow.

Sophia stared, stunned. The house was massive, the kind of place you'd see in glossy architecture magazines, not somewhere she'd imagined herself ending up tonight. She couldn't help but wonder how much money he had, what kind of life he lived outside of the boardroom. Did he really need *her* company?

Her gaze shifted to Carter, who seemed entirely at ease as the car came to a stop. He turned to her, a faint smile, but she saw something else in his eyes, something almost... tentative. "You okay?" he asked quietly.

She nodded, even though she wasn't sure what she felt. "Yeah, just... wow."

He chuckled, the sound low and a little self-conscious. "Yeah, it's a bit much, isn't it?"

"A bit?" she echoed, unable to keep the disbelief out of her voice. "Carter, this place is incredible."

He shrugged, looking almost sheepish. "It's just a house."

She shot him an incredulous look. "This is not *just* a house. This is a mansion."

"Technically, I think they call it a 'modern estate,'" he said, his tone light, teasing. "But I don't spend much time thinking about it."

"Clearly," she muttered, shaking her head. It was hard to wrap her mind around the scale of it all. How many rooms did one person need? And why would someone with this much wealth even bother with something as risky and exhausting as a corporate takeover?

The Uber driver opened the door, and Carter stepped out, then turned to offer her his hand. She took it, feeling a strange jolt of warmth at the contact. He helped her out of the car, his grip steady and reassuring, and then they were standing there together, in front of what looked like an actual palace. She took a deep breath, trying to shake off the nerves fluttering in her stomach.

He led her up the stone steps to the massive front door, his hand resting lightly on her back. "I'm glad you came," he said softly as they paused in front of the entrance.

She glanced at him, surprised by the sincerity in his voice. "Are you?"

He nodded, his expression serious. "Yeah, I am."

He opened the door and gestured for her to step inside. The interior was as breathtaking as the exterior—high ceilings, chic lines, and walls of glass that offered an unobstructed view of the city lights twinkling far below. Despite the modern design, the space felt surprisingly warm, with plush furniture and soft lighting that made it feel more like a home than she'd expected.

"Wow," she said again, unable to come up with anything more articulate.

Carter laughed, a genuine, relaxed sound that made her heart do a little flip. "You keep saying that."

She turned to him, raising an eyebrow. "I'm sorry, am I supposed to be jaded about walking into a billionaire's palace?"

"It's not a palace," he said, sounding faintly exasperated.

"It kind of is," she insisted, unable to help the smile that tugged at her lips. "Does the staff curtsy when you walk by?" *The wine must be talking.*

He groaned, but she could see the amusement in his eyes. "No one curtsies, and there's no staff right now. Just me. And you." He paused as he looked at her. "I'm glad you're here, Sophia. Really."

There it was again, that sincerity that caught her off guard. She felt her smile fade a little, something warm and tentative blossoming in its place. "I'm glad, too," she said softly, and realized she meant it.

He held her gaze for a long moment, then seemed to shake himself. "Come on," he said, his voice lightening. "Let's get some wine. It's been a long night."

He led her through the house, and she followed, trying to take it all in. The living room was expansive, with floor-to-ceiling windows that looked out over the city. She could just make out the faint glitter of the bay in the distance, the lights of boats dotting the water. It was beautiful, almost overwhelming.

They moved into the kitchen, a space that somehow managed to be both sleek and welcoming. A large island dominated the center, and the countertops were lined with pristine white marble. She wasn't supposed to feel comfortable here, with him. But she did.

Carter pulled out a bottle of wine and poured them each a glass. He handed her one, their fingers brushing, and she felt a spark of something she couldn't quite name. She took a sip, the rich flavor warming her from the inside out.

"You looked like you were ready to kill me when I first showed up tonight," he said, a teasing note in his voice. "I wasn't sure if I was going to survive the night."

She couldn't help but smile. "I might still change my mind. You're lucky you brought wine to bribe me."

He grinned, leaning against the counter, his posture relaxed. "So that's the secret. Wine, and you won't murder me."

"Well, it helps," she said with a mock-serious nod. "But I'll need a lot more than one glass."

He laughed, the sound filling the space around them, and she felt a surprising sense of ease settle over her. This was nice. Just talking, bantering.

"So, wine is your weakness," he said, his eyes gleaming with playful challenge. "What else do I need to know?"

She pretended to think. "I have a soft spot for cheesy disaster movies. You know, the ones where every possible catastrophe happens all at once?"

He raised an eyebrow. "Like *Sharknado*?"

She laughed, shaking her head. "Even better. *The Day After Tomorrow*. Where it snows in New Delhi and wolves somehow survive a superstorm."

"That one?" He chuckled. "I guess it has its charm. Though I'd argue that *Armageddon* has the best ridiculous premise. Drilling into an asteroid to save the world? Classic."

She rolled her eyes, smiling. "Okay, I'll give you that one. It's so absurd, but it's impossible to look away."

"Sounds like we need a disaster movie marathon," he teased. "I've got a home theater upstairs that's perfect for mocking bad CGI and plot holes."

She raised an eyebrow, amused. "And popcorn?"

"Absolutely. I may know how to make a mean bowl of popcorn."

"Fancy," she said, her voice light, playful. "I might take you up on that."

She took another sip of her wine, glancing around the kitchen. "I'm surprised. I thought your place would be more... I don't know, cold? Impersonal?"

He tilted his head, his expression curious. "Why's that?"

"I don't know," she admitted. "I guess I just pictured you in some ultra-modern, glass-and-steel bachelor pad. Everything in black and white, nothing out of place."

He laughed softly, shaking his head. "I tried that once. It felt like I was living in a catalog. I needed a place that felt more... real."

She glanced around again, taking in the warm tones and comfortable furniture. "Well, you succeeded. This place is beautiful."

"Thank you," he said, his voice quiet. "It's the first place I've ever really thought of as home."

His words, so simple and sincere, made something in her chest tighten. She was starting to see a side of him that was different from the relentless businessman she'd been clashing with. Maybe there was more to him than she'd realized.

"Okay, now it's your turn," she said, a small smile playing on her lips. "What's something about you I wouldn't know?"

Carter shifted thoughtfully before he spoke. "I always wanted to renovate a house."

Sophia blinked, surprised. "Really? Why? This place is already so beautiful."

He chuckled softly. "It is, but I didn't do it with my own two hands. I've always thought learning how to renovate a home would be satisfying. Building something from scratch, fixing things—creating something that lasts. But I grew up in boardrooms and conference calls. Never really had the chance to get my hands dirty."

"Well, couldn't you buy a house and do that now?" she asked, raising an eyebrow.

He shook his head, a rueful smile on his lips. "No time. Running a company tends to eat up your schedule."

"Wow, that's unexpected," she said, genuinely intrigued. The image of Carter, all suited up and making deals, didn't quite fit with the idea of him in a tool belt, hammering away at a fixer-upper. "I would've never guessed."

He shrugged, a self-deprecating smile on his lips. "I guess there's more to me than spreadsheets and stock options."

She studied him for a moment, seeing the flicker of something vulnerable in his eyes. "You know, I think you'd be great at it. You've got an eye for detail, and you're persistent—probably a bit of a perfectionist too."

He laughed, the sound warm and genuine. "Maybe one day I'll give it a shot."

"Let's toast," he said suddenly, breaking the moment. He raised his glass, a playful glint in his eye. "To cheesy disaster movies and home makeovers."

She smiled, clinking her glass against his. "And to not murdering you. Yet."

Sophia laughed as they made their way from the kitchen to the living room, each carrying a fresh glass of wine. It was late—really late—but she didn't care. For the first time in ages, she felt relaxed, almost carefree. The world outside, with all its pressures and complications, seemed far away.

They sank into the plush couch, and she kicked off her shoes, curling her legs beneath her. The room was dimly lit, the soft glow of the fireplace casting flickering shadows on the walls. It felt cozy, intimate, as if they were in their own little bubble, insulated from everything else.

"So, ideal destinations," Carter said, turning to face her. "Where would you go if you could drop everything right now?"

She took a sip of her wine, considering. "That's easy. I've always wanted to see the Northern Lights. It's at the top of my bucket list."

He nodded thoughtfully. "I've been to Iceland. It's incredible, but I spent most of my time in meetings. Maybe I should go back and actually see it this time."

Sophia raised an eyebrow, her lips curving into a teasing smile. "Are you saying you'd take a vacation? I'm not sure I believe you."

"With the right company, maybe," he said, smirking. "I hear they make good daiquiris in Reykjavik."

She laughed, the sound bright and genuine. "I'd like to see you behind the bar. Shaking cocktails and wearing one of those ridiculous Hawaiian shirts."

"Hey, I can pull off a Hawaiian shirt," he said, pretending to look offended. "I'd be the best-dressed bartender in Iceland."

"Now *that's* something I'd pay to see," she teased, feeling a lightness she hadn't felt in a long time. It was strange how easily he could make her laugh, how natural it felt to be here with him, talking about dreams and vacations like they were just two normal people, not adversaries in some high-stakes corporate game. She couldn't think about work right now. She had to think of anything *but* work.

She took another sip of wine, watching him over the rim of her glass. There was something different about him tonight, something she hadn't seen before.

They talked about places they wanted to visit—he mentioned the Maldives, and she joked about how she'd probably spend the whole time hiding under an umbrella, avoiding the sun. He laughed, and she realized she loved the sound of it, deep and genuine, like it came from somewhere real.

"Never took you for the beach-type. You seem like you've gotta be busy 24/7."

He shrugged, a little sheepish. "I guess I am. But I'm trying to be better about that. To take a step back every now and then."

"Really?" she asked, surprised. "What brought that on?"

He hesitated. "You could say I had a bit of a wake-up call recently. Realized I was missing out on... well, a lot."

He was still intense, but there was a new softness too, an openness that drew her in.

"Why did you come tonight?" Sophia asked, breaking the silence. "You could've waited until morning to talk."

Carter shifted, looking almost raw. He glanced away before replying, "Seems like a good cause."

She studied him, then nodded. "It is. It's close to home."

"How so?" he asked gently.

"My grandmother," she said softly. "She has Alzheimer's. It's been awful to watch her slip away. I just... I wanted to do something, to fix it, you know?"

Carter's expression softened, a flicker of sadness crossing his face. Before she could say more, he leaned in, and, unexpectedly, his lips met hers.

"Carter, what are we doing?" she whispered, her heart pounding.

"I don't know," he murmured, his focus never leaving her. "But I don't want to stop."

Before she could think, before she could talk herself out of it, he was leaning in, and then his lips were on hers—soft, insistent, sending a rush of heat through her that made everything else fade away. She responded instinctively, her hands finding his shoulders as the kiss deepened, his arms wrapping around her as if he couldn't get close enough.

It was intoxicating, the feel of him, the taste of him. Her fingers threaded through his hair, and she sighed against his mouth, lost in the sensation. The world outside disappeared, leaving only the two of them, the heat and urgency building between them.

The kiss turned into more, their wine forgotten as they pressed closer. His hands moved to her waist, pulling her against him, and she felt herself melting into him. She couldn't think, couldn't breathe. All she knew was that she wanted more—more of him, more of this.

She broke the kiss, gasping for air, but he didn't let go, his forehead resting against hers. "Stay," he whispered, his voice rough with need. "Please."

She hesitated, the rational part of her brain screaming that this was a terrible idea, that she was crossing lines she couldn't uncross. But the way he was looking at her, the way he was holding her, like she was the only thing keeping him anchored—it was too much, too overwhelming to resist.

"Okay," she breathed, and his eyes darkened, a look of raw desire crossing his face.

He lifted her effortlessly, and she wrapped her arms around his neck, her pulse hammering as he carried her toward the bedroom. Her heart raced with a mix of anticipation and fear, but she didn't pull back. She didn't want to. Not tonight.

The door shut behind them.

CHAPTER 16

The knock on the door jolted Carter awake. He blinked, disoriented, sunlight streaming through the curtains, flooding the room with a soft, golden light. His head felt fuzzy, and for a moment, he couldn't remember why he felt so... relaxed. And then it hit him—the memory of last night, of Sophia in his arms, her laughter, her warmth, the way she'd looked at him with something that felt achingly close to trust.

But now, the bed was empty.

He sat up, sheets falling away. She was gone. No note, no trace —just cold emptiness. Usually, he was the one to leave, or made sure the woman was on her way out. But now? Was he actually *disappointed*? He'd thought this morning might be different, that they'd talk, maybe have breakfast together. Guess not. And *damn*, that stung more than he'd like to admit..

Another knock, this one louder, more insistent, echoed through the house. *Who the hell could that be at this hour?* He glanced at the clock. It was early—too early for visitors, especially uninvited ones.

He grabbed a shirt from the floor, pulling it on as he headed downstairs, his mind still half on Sophia, on the way she'd smiled at him, the way her eyes had softened when she talked.

He swung the door open, his expression darkening when he saw Eleanor standing there, her lips curled into a smug smile. She looked annoyingly put-together, as always, her hair perfectly styled, her suit immaculate. She pushed her sunglasses up into her hair and raised an eyebrow at him.

"Well, good morning to you, too," she said, her voice dripping with sarcasm. "Whose car or Uber did I pass on my way up here? Didn't think you'd have company this early."

"What do you want, Eleanor?"

"Well, I tried to reach you. You're usually up early, but you didn't answer. We have a big breakfast with our new CEO, David. Didn't want you to miss it."

"I'm not going to breakfast, and I'm not backing David," he snapped.

Eleanor rolled her eyes. "We've been over this, Carter. Breakfast is at 9 a.m. sharp. Get dressed—you smell like you've been drinking."

He felt it too, but he wasn't backing down. "I'm not going to breakfast!" he shouted as she turned to leave.

"Yes, you are!" she mocked back. "And I'm bringing Kyle."

"You can't bring your fiancé to a business breakfast." He hollered after her.

She smirked, shutting the door behind her. "I have to. We're tasting cake right after. Bye."

She slammed the door. *Oh, this was bad.*

He'd promised Sophia he had nothing to do with David and that he'd fix it. Even mentioned the small error that could get her out of this. Now Eleanor was dragging him to breakfast— which was the last thing he needed after last night. *Oh shit,* did that really happen, or was it just a crazy, sex dream?

He ran a hand over his face, groaning. He'd definitely had too much to drink, but inviting her to his place... yeah, he knew what he was doing. But then she'd just disappeared the next morning. Did she regret it?

His phone chirped, snapping him out of his thoughts. His assistant. "Grant Technologies' attorneys want to meet ASAP about the legality of the documents. They said it's urgent."

Perfect. A way out. He wasn't going to breakfast. "Set it up with Joshua," he replied, already grabbing his jacket. Time to get to the office. He paused, then added, "And set a meeting with Jack Porter. He owes me one."

CHAPTER 17

Sophia had slipped out of Carter's place early that morning. He looked so peaceful sleeping that she hadn't wanted to wake him. Besides, she needed to get ready for her meeting with Joshua.

Back at home, she jumped into the shower, the hot water helping to clear her head a little. Afterward, she poured herself some coffee, wincing as the headache from last night's drinks made itself known. *Ouch.*

As the hot water poured over her, she closed her eyes, trying to sort through the tangle of thoughts and feelings. Last night felt unreal. Carter wasn't just charming; he was unexpectedly kind, human. It twisted her heart in ways she hadn't anticipated.

"Get a grip, Sophia," she muttered under her breath, scrubbing shampoo through her hair a bit too vigorously. "He's still the guy trying to take over your company. Don't get distracted just because he has a smile that could probably charm the pants off a statue."

She let the water soothe her, wishing the connection with Carter wasn't just a fantasy. Believing in them felt dangerous.

She stepped out of the shower and wrapped herself in a towel, catching sight of her reflection in the mirror. Her cheeks were flushed, her eyes bright, and she looked... different. Vulnerable, almost. She frowned at herself and shook her head.

"This is ridiculous," she said aloud, brushing her hair with quick, decisive strokes. "It was one night. Get over it. You have a company to save."

In the kitchen, she made a cup of coffee, her usual morning ritual, hoping the familiar routine would ground her. She grabbed her phone, her thumb hovering over the screen, a small part of her hoping to see a message from him. But there was nothing. Not a single word.

"Well, what did you expect?" she muttered to herself, pouring cream into her cup. "A love letter? Maybe a poem or two?" She rolled her eyes, forcing a lightness she didn't quite feel. "It was just one night, Sophia. Pull yourself together."

She glanced at her phone again, irritation flaring when she realized she was still hoping to see his name pop up on the screen. "Ugh," she told herself firmly, setting the phone down with a thud. "He's probably already back to plotting how to take over your company. Stop acting like a lovesick teenager."

It wasn't like she hadn't been through this before. She knew better than to trust too easily, to let her guard down. She'd spent years building up walls, becoming the woman who could stand toe-to-toe with the likes of Carter. But last night... she definitely wasn't toe to toe.

"Okay," she said, taking a deep breath. "Enough of this. You have a job to do." She finished her coffee and headed upstairs to get dressed, pulling on her usual business attire like armor.

But as she gathered her things, preparing to leave, she found herself glancing at her phone one last time. Still nothing. Fine. If he wanted to play it cool, she could do the same. Okay... maybe he's still sleeping. *Chill out.*

Sophia called Joshua on her way to work. "Did you read the paperwork?"

"Yes," he replied. "It's pretty airtight. If David has the majority shares and the board signed, there's not much I can do. We can tie them up in litigation, but it might get expensive."

Her grip tightened on the steering wheel. Carter had mentioned something about a small detail that could unravel the paperwork, but she couldn't remember exactly what he said—or if she'd imagined the whole thing. She had a lot of drinks last night. "David has to be in some kind of trouble. It doesn't make sense for him to do this. Maybe his divorce with Becky was worse than I thought—maybe she took everything."

She made a mental note to reach out to Becky, hoping she could shed some light. Joshua sighed. "I'll dig into David's situation, but it's effective immediately, Sophia. Technically, you don't have a job to go to."

The words hit her. She hadn't even caught that in the paperwork. How could they do this to her? She was a good boss—loyal. How did David convince them to sign? It didn't add up.

"Listen, I've already set up a meeting with Carter this morning," Joshua said. "Do you think there's a play there?"

So Carter *was* awake. "He said it was Eleanor who brought David in, not him." She wanted to believe that was true.

"I can work with that," Joshua replied.

She hung up and immediately called Becky.

No answer. Why would she pick up? They were never close, but she'd thought they were at least friends. Frustrated, she dialed Jessica next. She needed answers—why the hell would Jessica sign those documents?

Nothing. Straight to voicemail.

Her phone rang, and she glanced at the screen. Becky. She took a deep breath and answered. "Hi! I really hope we can talk."

CHAPTER 18

Carter stared at the documents spread across his desk, but something didn't add up. The pieces weren't fitting together, and it gnawed at him like a splinter under his skin. He was distracted by his phone buzzing—a text from an old flame. Sarah wanted to swing by and grab lunch. He fired off a quick reply: *Can't today, busy,* and brushed it aside.

His eyes drifted back to the papers, scanning them with fresh focus. Oh yes, he remembered —the small error buried in the fine print, barely noticeable. It was the same mistake a competitor had once overlooked in a deal years ago, a mistake that had nullified the entire agreement and cost him millions. It was burned into his memory.

The error was obvious, and even their legal team missed it. He still wanted Grant Technologies, just not with David as CEO. He'd mentioned it to Sophia last night, but everything was a blur. Maybe she hadn't heard him or realized what it meant.

Just then, Eleanor and David walked into his office, Kyle trailing behind them. Eleanor's voice was sugary sweet. "You missed a lovely breakfast, but we're pulling HR in for some onboarding this morning. We'd appreciate it if you could join us, Carter."

"I can't right now," he replied.

Eleanor's eyes narrowed with frustration. "Kyle, David, can I have a moment with Carter?" she said, her tone clipped.

They exchanged glances before stepping out of the office, leaving Eleanor and Carter alone.

"What the hell is going on with you?" she hissed as soon as the door closed. "We have a company to wrap up, and you're acting really weird."

"I don't know how many times I have to tell you that I don't trust David," Carter shot back. "We're not moving forward with him. We can still finish this deal, but with Sophia as CEO. I don't do business like this."

"It's a done deal, Carter," she snapped. "The documents are signed."

"No, it's not," he said, pulling the documents from his desk. "You didn't cross your T's and dot your I's, Eleanor. There's an error on the paperwork and this shows me you don't have what it takes. Running behind my back on our first deal was a huge mistake. I'm done with this childish business behavior."

"What are you talking about?" she demanded.

He shook his head. "Doesn't matter. These documents are null."

Eleanor's eyes flashed. "Then make them *not* null. You're going to make me look bad."

"That's on you, little sis," Carter replied coolly. "You should know better than to pull stunts like this. We don't do shady deals."

"Oh, so we just tell David to go home?" she shot back. "That could blow up the whole deal. We lose the board's confidence, we plant doubt, and we look like we don't have our shit together. Is *that* how we do business, Carter?"

"We'll have to figure something out," Carter said, rubbing his head. "If we start this deal with David, it's going to sink fast."

Eleanor rolled her eyes. "Well, we better figure it out quickly. Until then, I'm moving forward with HR."

She turned to leave, but he held up a hand, trying to think clearly. She was right—they had to handle this delicately to avoid losing the board's confidence.

Just then, a notification popped up. Sarah again. *Hey Carter, I'm in the lobby, ready for lunch.*

A second later, his phone was flashing Sarah's name on his screen.

He let out a frustrated sigh. *Ugh.*

CHAPTER 19

"Okay, I'll meet." Becky said cautiously. They agreed to meet at a small coffee shop across town.

When Sophia arrived, she spotted Becky immediately. She looked rough—exhausted, with dark circles under her eyes and a tension that seemed to radiate from the center of her back. After a few awkward pleasantries, Sophia decided to cut to the chase.

"I know this is uncomfortable, but I have to ask—why is David suddenly interested in the company he never gave a damn about?"

Becky sighed heavily, slumping back in her chair. "The divorce was brutal, but it's over now."

Sophia hovered forward, her voice gentle. "What happened?"

Her expression hardened, bitterness creeping into her eyes. "I caught him cheating. With some woman from his office. She was filling his head with these ideas about getting into business, building an empire together—like some twisted corporate Bonnie and Clyde fantasy."

Sophia's stomach churned. "What kind of person would do that?"

"The kind who preys on easy targets," Becky replied, her voice laced with resentment. "And David took the bait. He's got a gambling problem, Sophia. And a drinking one. He's drowning in debt. Took out loans for God knows what, and now the creditors are coming for him."

Sophia's mind raced as the pieces clicked into place. "So he's trying to take over the company to bail himself out. He needs the money."

Becky nodded, her gaze weary and defeated. "Yeah. He's desperate. It's like he thinks grabbing control will solve everything."

Sophia reached across the table and squeezed Becky's hand. "I'm so sorry you had to go through all this. Thank you for being honest with me. If you need anything, I'm here."

Becky gave her a small, sad smile, the weariness in her eyes softening just a bit. "Thanks, Sophia. I appreciate it."

They finished their coffee, and as Sophia stepped out of the café, her phone buzzed. *Jessica.* She took a deep breath, her hand tightening around her bag as she answered. "How could you sign those documents, Jess? I thought we were friends."

"We are," Jessica said, her voice cracking with emotion. "I'm so sorry, Sophia."

"Then why would you betray me? I would've never done that to you. And behind my back? What reason could you possibly have?"

Jessica's voice trembled. "I'm really sorry, but you don't know the whole story."

"Then explain," Sophia demanded, frustration bubbling over.

"I'd rather do it in person," Jessica whispered.

Sophia clenched her jaw, her frustration simmering. "Fine. When?"

They agreed to meet later, and Sophia hung up, her mind racing. As if on cue, her phone rang again—Joshua this time.

"I just met with Carter," he said. "He was cooperative, but the paperwork is solid. For now, David's the CEO."

Sophia's blood boiled. "Carter said he'd fix this! And now it's a done deal?"

She ended the call and, still fuming, decided to confront Carter herself. As she stepped into the lobby of his building, she noticed a beautiful woman, perfectly put-together, dialing her phone. They both got into the elevator, and the woman's voice carried through the small space.

"Hey, it's Sarah. I'm here for lunch, Carter. See you soon, babe."

Sophia's stomach dropped. *Sarah. Babe?* She stayed silent, letting Sarah exit the elevator alone. *Seriously?* He was meeting another woman for lunch—after everything that happened between them last night? Maybe he really was just full of shit.

Her heart tightened as she felt a fresh wave of betrayal. Had Carter just used her to get her into bed? Pretended to care about her event, about her? Outrage twisted inside her as the elevator doors closed, shutting out the world.

CHAPTER 20

"Hey, it's Sarah. I'm here for lunch, Carter. See you soon, babe." Here voice came through the phone.

Carter pinched the bridge of his nose, irritation flaring. "I told you, Sarah, I'm in the middle of something. I don't want to give you the wrong idea—I'm seeing someone else."

Her voice turned stern. "But, Carter?"

"It's been over a month, Sarah. Stop trying to drop in on me."

There was a pause, then she sounded almost defeated. "You're seeing someone?"

He hesitated, then decided to be honest. "Yes, actually. She's pretty special."

There was silence on the line, then a quiet click as she hung up. Carter sighed, leaning back in his chair. *Close call.*

He dialed Jack Porter. "Any updates for me?"

"Yes, actually. Quite a few," Jack replied. "I'll meet you shortly."

Carter hung up and, without thinking, called Sophia. He'd been replaying last night in his head all morning, wondering why she'd slipped out without a word. But the call went straight to voicemail.

He shot her a quick text: *Hope you're having a good day. I had a great time last night. Hope your head isn't hurting—mine is.*

He watched the screen, noticing the three dots appear, then disappear. Nothing. He tossed his phone on the desk with a sigh, running a hand through his hair. Something felt off, and the silence from her was unsettling.

Turning back to the documents, he skimmed over the fine print again. The small error he'd spotted earlier loomed large in his mind, and he knew it could be his leverage to shift things back in Sophia's favor. But how to play it?

Just then, his office door opened, and Jack walked in. Dressed impeccably as always, his expression was serious as he set his briefcase down and took a seat.

"Jack," Carter greeted, his tone urgent. "What have you got?"

Jack nodded, flipping open his case and pulling out a stack of papers. "A lot, actually. We need to talk strategy."

Jack, his private investigator, settled into the chair and spread out a stack of documents across Carter's desk. "This David guy is a real mess. Why do you need intel on him?"

Carter settled back, frustration evident in his eyes. "I've got a bad feeling. Eleanor's pushing him as the new CEO, but he's not right for it. I need to know what I'm dealing with."

Jack nodded, glancing over the papers. "Makes sense. From what I've found, he's got a messy divorce, gambling debts, an affair... and he started buying up shares right after you made your offer to take over Grant Technologies."

Carter's brows furrowed. "That's odd. How would he know to do that? The offer wasn't public."

Jack jutted forward, lowering his voice. "That's where it gets interesting. It looks like the person he was having an affair with was on the inside—maybe feeding him information."

Carter's mind spiraled. *Insider information. That's a legal nightmare.* "Do we know who it is?"

Jack shrugged. "I have my hunches, but nothing solid yet."

Carter exhaled. "This sounds like a scandal waiting to happen. I'm not sure I want to be a part of something this messy." He glanced at his phone, hoping for a reply from Sophia. Still nothing.

"We'd have a media nightmare if it got out that the newly appointed CEO was having an affair and had access to insider information," Carter continued, his tone grim. He looked back at Jack. "I should warn Eleanor. This has disaster written all over it."

Jack nodded, watching Carter closely. "What's your next move?"

Carter's expression was tense. "I need to get Sophia back as CEO without this whole thing blowing up. But I've got something that might help." He slid the documents across the desk to Jack. "Take a look."

Jack, an ex-attorney, examined the papers, his eyes widening as he read through them. "Oh, this tactic. Didn't Platon use something like this against you a few years back?"

"Yeah," Carter said, a bitter smile forming. "Cost me a fortune. I never forgot it."

Jack nodded, impressed. "It's a small detail, but it's powerful. If we use it right, it could nullify the takeover documents."

"Exactly," Carter agreed. "I need to figure out how to play this without blowing everything up. Sophia deserves better than what she's getting, and David isn't the right guy to lead this company."

Carter relaxed back, his mind churning. "Okay, how do we get David out without the board losing faith and without causing chaos?"

Jack tapped his fingers on the desk thoughtfully. "Well, we could start by exposing his financial instability. The board won't back a CEO who's drowning in debt and has a gambling problem. We'd have to be discreet, though. Make it look like we're acting in the company's best interest, not just trying to get rid of him."

"True, but that could make the board question their own decision-making. We need something less scandalous, more strategic," Carter said, rubbing his chin.

"What if we convince the board that David lacks the necessary experience?" Jack suggested. "We could create a narrative that he's not equipped to handle the company's complexities. Highlight his lack of corporate experience and compare it to Sophia's track record. Make them see it's a safer bet to reinstate her."

Carter nodded slowly. "That's better. We could propose a co-CEO arrangement with Sophia, just to ease him out gradually."

Jack raised an eyebrow. "Sophia as co-CEO, then transition David into a different role, maybe something less visible. If he screws up there, we have grounds to remove him entirely."

"Or," Carter said, an idea sparking, "we could spin it as a health concern. Talk up the stress and responsibility of the role, suggesting David should focus on himself and his well-being. If he's struggling personally, the board might see stepping down as the best option for everyone."

Jack smirked. "Or we could plant the idea that David stepping aside now, gracefully, could preserve his reputation and even open up future opportunities for him elsewhere."

Carter nodded thoughtfully. "That's not bad. And if we get David to voluntarily step down, it looks like a win-win. No scandal, no board drama, and we bring Sophia back as the natural choice."

Jack crossed his arms. "The key is to frame it right. We make it about protecting the company and David, not just booting him out."

"Agreed," Carter said, a sense of clarity forming. "We need to handle this carefully, but it's possible."

Carter's eyes narrowed. "What if we get David to step down voluntarily? Let him know we're aware of his scandal—the affair, the insider information. He might be desperate enough to walk away without a fight."

Jack nodded slowly. "That might be our best option. We keep it quiet, avoid a public mess, and get the board on our side. If he feels cornered, he'll probably want to protect what's left of his reputation."

"Exactly," Carter said, a hint of relief in his voice. "If we can make him see that stepping down is his only way out, we avoid blowing everything up. Then we pitch Sophia to the board as the obvious choice for CEO."

Jack leaned back, considering. "It's risky, but if we handle it right, we can make this whole thing look like David's decision. The board won't feel blindsided, and they'll likely back Sophia if she seems like the stabilizing force in all this."

Carter nodded. "And David saves face. Everyone wins. If we play our cards right, we can turn this mess around."

Jack grinned. "And you get Sophia back where she belongs—at the head of the company."

Carter's expression softened. "It's not just about that. It's about making things right." He glanced at the documents again, determination in his eyes. "Let's make this happen."

CHAPTER 21

Sophia stood in the lobby, feeling like a complete fool. *Of course,* she thought bitterly. *Women practically throw themselves at Carter Kane.* And of course, he already had someone else lined up—another woman ready to fill whatever role he needed. He was a player, and she'd been stupid enough to think there was something real between them.

She clenched her fists, replaying everything he'd said. He promised to fix things, but Joshua had just told her David as CEO was practically a done deal. This was his plan all along, wasn't it? To take over her company and destroy everything her father had built. And all that talk about Eleanor working with David behind his back—total bullshit. *It had to be.* It was probably Carter's idea from the start.

All flash, no substance, she fumed. Beneath that smooth exterior was something rotten. Just like Evan. She should've known better than to fall for it again.

But she wasn't going to roll over and let him take everything from her. She might not have a job to go to today, but she still had fight left in her. She was going to figure out what had really happened, starting with why Jessica, her supposed friend and COO, would sign those documents.

Sophia gripped the steering wheel. Carter's smooth charm replayed in her head, fueling her irritation. How could she have been so naïve? No more tears. She needed answers, and she was going to get them.

When she pulled up to Jessica's apartment, she took a deep

breath, forcing herself to calm down. The sleek building, with its modern architecture and meticulously landscaped entrance, felt almost surreal, like a place that had no business hosting the confrontation she knew was about to unfold.

She rang Jessica's unit, and after a few tense moments, the door swung open. Jessica stood there, her eyes red and swollen, as if she'd been crying.

"Why aren't you in the office today?" Sophia asked, the words tumbling out before she could stop them. Her anger was a thin veil over her concern.

Jessica blinked, looking momentarily stunned. "I, um, needed a day," she said, her voice shaky.

Sophia's heart twisted, a flicker of a memory flashing through her mind. There was a time, not so long ago, when they would spend hours in Jessica's living room, laughing over glasses of wine and talking about their dreams for the company. They'd been more than colleagues—they'd been friends. Sophia had trusted Jessica to be her right hand, her confidante. And now this?

The bitterness returned, and she forced herself to focus on the present. "A day?" Sophia snapped, stepping inside. "You signed the takeover documents behind my back, Jess. You didn't even give me a heads up. I thought we were *friends*. I trusted you with everything, and this is how you repay me?"

Jessica's face fell as she closed the door behind them. "Sophia, I'm so sorry. I wanted to tell you, but—"

"But what?" Sophia interrupted, her voice trembling with hurt. "You thought it would be better to just go behind my back and sell me out?"

Jessica bit her lip, her eyes filling with fresh tears. "I'll tell you everything, I promise. Just... Please, hear me out."

Before Sophia could respond, a noise came from her pocket. She pulled out her phone and saw Carter's name flashing on the screen. Rage flared in her chest, and she immediately sent the call to voicemail. *That asshole.*

A second later, a text came through: *Hope you're doing okay. I'd love to talk if you're up for it.*

Sophia almost laughed out loud, the absurdity of it all hitting her like a punch to the gut. *Probably having lunch with another woman while texting me,* she thought bitterly. She shoved her phone back into her pocket and turned her attention to Jessica.

Jessica had returned with two glasses of water, setting them on the coffee table before sitting down on the couch. She looked exhausted, like she'd aged overnight.

"It started out innocently," Jessica whispered, her voice trembling. "We met at a networking event. He looked familiar, and... well, it was David, your brother."

"What?" Sophia's voice rose, shock and confusion lacing her words.

"I know," Jessica said, shame coloring her cheeks. "He was married, and it really was innocent at first, I swear. He asked about you, about the company. We met for a drink, and I don't know... we just started talking more and more. And before I knew it, I was madly in love with him. God, I'm so embarrassed."

Sophia's stomach churned. "You had an affair with David?"

Jessica's eyes widened, and she shook her head furiously. "I thought he was separated! He told me he and Becky were done. I believed him, Sophia. He said he wanted to be with me, that he was interested in the company because he wanted to be a part of your life again."

The pieces were clicking into place. "So *you're* the one who fed him information?"

Jessica's eyes filled with tears. "I didn't mean to. I just thought he was being supportive. He kept asking questions, and I didn't think—"

"Didn't think?" Sophia cut her off, her voice sharp. "You handed him everything on a silver platter, and now he's using it to take me down."

"Are you still seeing David?" Sophia demanded.

Jessica shook her head, tears brimming. "Not after he blackmailed me into signing those documents. He threatened to tell everyone I was leaking inside information. He said if I didn't get the board on his side, I'd go to prison. I'm so sorry, Sophia!" She broke down, covering her face with her hands. "I stood by him through his divorce, thinking we were going to be together. He told me he was leaving her for me!"

"He didn't leave her, Jess. She found out about you and *she* filed for divorce."

Jessica's face drained of color, disbelief washing over her. "*That liar*! I don't know what to do. I'm ashamed, and I don't want to go to prison. I helped him sway the board, and I feel horrible."

Sophia was silent, stunned by the betrayal. She swallowed, trying to process. "You know this could get you in serious trouble, right? David buying shares with insider knowledge could ruin both of you."

Jessica nodded, her voice breaking. "I know, but I swear, I didn't know he was buying shares. I had no idea he was interested in the company. He saw an opportunity and took it, and I was just... I was stupid."

Sophia took a deep breath, trying to think clearly. "Is there anything you can do to help fix this? Because if not, the police might be the only way to get David out."

Jessica's eyes widened in panic. "No, please! Don't go to the police. I'll lose everything. I can't go to jail!"

Sophia's voice was firm. "I'm not taking the fall for your mistakes, Jess. You lied to me. You went behind my back and helped him, and now my company is at risk. I'm not losing everything because you couldn't see through his bullshit."

Jessica's face crumpled. "There's something else you should know."

Sophia shook her head, her voice tight. "Frankly, Jessica, I've heard enough."

"Please, it's important," Jessica pleaded, her eyes brimming with desperation.

But Sophia had reached her limit. She grabbed her bag, her hands trembling with resentment and hurt. "I think I've heard all I need to hear," she snapped, her voice shaking. "I can't believe you would do this."

Jessica took a step forward, but Sophia was already heading for the door, her back rigid, her heart pounding. She didn't look back, didn't slow down. The betrayal was too raw, too painful to let Jessica's words reach her.

CHAPTER 22

Carter checked his phone again. Still nothing from Sophia. He had called and texted a few times—no response. Frustration and disappointment settled in his chest like a heavy weight. He couldn't stop replaying last night in his mind, the way she'd felt in his arms, how real it had seemed. But now? Not a word.

He went home to his quiet mansion, its grand size feeling more like a burden than a luxury. Evidence of last night lingered—her wine glass on the counter, the faint scent of her perfume. He could still feel the warmth of her kiss, the softness of her touch. *What happened?*

Dropping his things by the door, he couldn't stay in the emptiness. He grabbed his keys and headed to the nursing home.

The on-site nurse met him as he arrived. "Mr. Kane, your father's been declining the past few days. He's been more confused than usual."

Carter's heart tightened, and he nodded. "Thanks for letting me know."

He made his way down the familiar hallway to his dad's room. The smell of antiseptic hung in the air, and a TV droned softly in the background. His father sat in a recliner, staring blankly at the wall.

"Hey, Dad," he said softly, trying to sound upbeat. "It's me, Carter."

His dad's eyes flickered over to him, confusion clouding his features. "Carter?" he murmured, the name foreign on his lips. "I don't... I don't know any Carter."

Carter's chest ached, but he forced a smile. "That's okay, Dad. I'm just here to see how you're doing."

His father frowned, lost in some memory or maybe nothing at all. Carter tried to engage him, talking about the weather, the football game he knew his dad used to love, but there was no response—just that vacant, heartbreaking stare.

His phone vibrated in his pocket, and he glanced at the screen. David. Finally. He took a deep breath and stepped into the quiet lobby to answer.

"David, thanks for calling me back," Carter began, his tone tense and direct. "I think we need to come to an agreement about your involvement with the company."

"That's already been figured out," David responded coolly. "I'm the new CEO, and I have the majority share. There's nothing to agree on, Carter."

"Do you know what insider trading is, David?" he asked, his voice low and dangerous. "It's when someone uses non-public, material information to make trades, which is not only unethical but illegal. And guess what? That's exactly what you've been doing."

"You can't prove that," David shot back, his voice laced with arrogance. "This is my family's business. I have every right to purchase shares and claim my stake."

"Sure, if that were true," Carter replied, "but you had no interest in Grant Technologies until you started buying shares right when Kane Enterprises made an offer. An offer that wasn't public. The timing seems pretty coincidental, don't you think?"

David scoffed. "There's no proof. How would I get that kind of information anyway? You've got no leg to stand on, Carter. I just have good timing, that's all."

"I know you've been having an affair," Carter pressed, his voice cold. "I just don't know with who yet. Maybe someone on the inside?"

"Lies. All lies," David snapped, his denial immediate. "I've never cheated. You have no idea what you're talking about."

"You had a pretty messy divorce, David. It's all documented—your ex accused you of cheating on her."

David scoffed. "Again, no proof. Just my ex trying to get everything she could. I was nothing but a loyal husband. She took it all. My marriage is none of your damn business, Carter."

"Well, it is now, isn't it, David?" Carter's voice was icy. "I'm not getting tangled up in some insider trading scandal. You've got zero experience as a CEO and suddenly show up right before an acquisition?"

"Don't forget, I have the majority now," David shot back, his tone smug. "And the board's on *my* side. We don't need to be enemies, Carter. We can work together. I've got plans for Grant Enterprises that'll make us both a lot of money."

Carter's eyes narrowed as David continued, his voice dripping with confidence. "Think about what's important. If we join forces, I guarantee you'll love the profits coming your way."

Carter glanced up as a nurse approached, her expression serious. "Mr. Kane, I need to speak with you," she said quietly.

He sighed, still reeling from his conversation with David. "I've got to go," he said into the phone. "We can continue this tomorrow." He hung up, shoving the phone back into his pocket. There was no way he was joining forces with David. His gut told him this guy was trouble, and his instincts rarely failed.

Turning to the nurse, he asked, "What's going on?"

She hesitated, then said gently, "Your father's condition is declining. We're concerned he might need hospice care soon."

"Whatever he needs, I'll make sure it happens," Carter said, his voice rough. "Anything."

She nodded, offering a comforting smile before stepping aside as he walked into his dad's room. The place was quiet, the soft hum of machines and the faint scent of antiseptic filling the air. His father sat slumped in the chair, staring blankly out the window.

Carter's gaze fell on a stack of old photographs on the dresser. He picked them up, flipping through them slowly. "What are these? I've never seen them before," he asked the nurse, who had followed him in.

"Richard's brother, Bruce, dropped them off recently," she explained. "He's been visiting and brought these old photos for your dad to look through."

"Uncle Bruce?" Carter muttered, surprised. He hadn't talked to his uncle in years. "He's still around? Must be getting pretty old."

The nurse chuckled. "He's a character, that's for sure. He visits Richard often. They seem to really enjoy looking through these together."

Carter settled into a chair, flipping through the pictures. The early shots were mostly of his dad and Bruce—two brothers growing up, laughing, goofing around. There were some awkward teenage photos, prom pictures with dated tuxes, and candid vacation shots of his parents, his dad proudly rocking a bright Hawaiian shirt.

He smiled. As he turned to another picture, his breath caught. He stared at a photo of his father standing with another man who looked uncannily like David—same features, same piercing eyes. But the hair, the clothes, everything else screamed '80s. It was uncanny, like David had been teleported back in time.

Carter flipped the picture over and squinted at the faded blue ink on the back. It read, "Grant and Kane, 1982."

His stomach twisted. *What the hell?* He had been told their families were enemies, that his dad and James Grant had been at odds for years. James Grant was the one who ruined his reputation. But this? This looked like two friends. Two business partners. Maybe even allies.

He stared at the photo. Everything he thought he knew was unraveling. Maybe he needed to connect with Uncle Bruce. Get some answers.

Carter's stomach growled, pulling him out of his thoughts. He realized he hadn't eaten all day. The idea of dinner—and seeing Sophia—crossed his mind. He needed to talk to her, even if he couldn't reveal everything just yet. There was too much at stake, and any slip could create a liability for Kane Enterprises.

He pulled out his phone, hesitating for a moment before texting her. He wanted to reassure her that he was working on it, that he hadn't given up. But how much could he say without making things worse?

His mind was focused on plans to get David out of the company. The scandal, the insider trading—it was all unsafe territory. If he pushed too hard, he could implicate Kane Enterprises. But if he didn't act, David would stay in control, and Grant Technologies would be a sinking ship.

He glanced at the photo again. His father and James Grant, side by side, looking like business partners instead of rivals. *What had really happened between them?* He needed answers, but right now, he needed to see Sophia more.

Taking a deep breath, he sent the message: *Hey, you free for dinner? I'd really like to see you.* He paused, then added, *I'm still working on things. Can't say too much, but I want you to know I'm doing everything I can.*

He hit send, hoping she would respond. He needed to see her face, needed her to understand that he was on her side, even if he couldn't lay all his cards on the table just yet.

CHAPTER 23

Sophia left Jessica's apartment, her head spinning. She could hardly believe what she'd just heard. A plan began to take shape in her mind. David thought he could waltz in and take over everything, but he didn't have a clue what he was doing. He wasn't a CEO. *She* was. And now was her chance to prove it.

She wasn't about to let David or Carter—or anyone—steal her company. She thought of her father and what he would do. He'd fight back, and so would she.

Needing some guidance, she decided to stop by her mom's house. Maybe her mom could offer some advice. After all, this was David they were talking about. Family.

She pulled up to her childhood house, its welcoming sight calming her nerves. Her mom greeted her at the door, and the comforting scent of home-cooked meatloaf wafted through the air. It had always been her favorite.

"Hey, honey," her mom said, pulling her in for a hug. "You look tired. Everything okay?"

"Do you have any wine, Mom?" Sophia asked. Promising herself that next week she would tone down the wine.

"Of course." Her mom gave her a concerned look but led her inside.

The living room was a time capsule of her childhood. Pictures of her and David as kids lined the walls, their parents' smiles beaming down at them. Everything felt so warm and safe, like it hadn't changed at all, even though her world had turned upside down.

They sat down with glasses of red wine, and Sophia took a deep breath. She needed to tell her mom everything. How David had betrayed her, how he was trying to take the company out from under her.

"I don't know what to do, Mom. David's trying to take everything Dad built, and I just feel... lost."

Her mom's eyes softened with concern. "I know, sweetheart. It's hard to believe he'd do something like this."

Sophia shook her head, frustration simmering beneath her calm exterior. "I never thought he cared about the company. Now he's acting like he's entitled to it. And the board is backing him. It's like I'm fighting a losing battle."

Her mom looked thoughtful for a moment, then set her glass down. "There's something I need to tell you. It's about your father and the company. It's... complicated."

Sophia frowned. "What do you mean?"

"Your dad had a plan, a vision for the company's future. But it wasn't just about you or David. It involved Carter Kane's father, too."

Sophia nearly choked on her wine. "Wait—what? Carter's dad? What does he have to do with anything? Carter mentioned they knew each other, but I didn't believe him."

Her mom took a deep breath. "Years ago, your father and Carter's father were more than just business rivals. They were actually friends. They even invested in a major project together, something that was supposed to revolutionize the tech industry. But it didn't go as planned."

"Why have I never heard about this?" Sophia's voice was laced with disbelief.

"It was a huge failure, Sophia. The project tanked, and it nearly bankrupted both families. The damage was so bad that they had a major falling out, and Richard swore he'd never speak to him again. But your dad... he never let go of the idea. He kept developing it, secretly, using Grant Technologies' resources."

Sophia blinked. "So, Dad was still working on it? Even after the fallout?"

"Yes," her mom continued. "And he set up a secret trust fund tied to that project's success. The idea was that if the technology ever took off, it would secure the family's future and stabilize the company no matter what. The trust fund is hidden within the company's financial structure, and it's worth a fortune—far more than anyone knows."

"Wait... there's a hidden trust fund?"

Her mom nodded. "Yes, and before he died, your father wrote a letter—a detailed plan for the company and the trust. It was meant for the board, to keep the company in the family and mend things with Carter's dad. He wanted to surprise Richard, prove he never gave up on their friendship. But he passed before he could share it."

Sophia's eyes widened. "Where is this letter?"

Her mom's expression clouded with regret. "It was supposed to be with his lawyer, but after your father died, it never surfaced. I think someone hid it or destroyed it."

Sophia stared at her mom, trying to process everything. "Why would someone hide it?"

"Because that letter would change everything," her mom said softly. "It laid out how the trust should be used and the company managed. Your dad always wanted *you* to run it—you were the one by his side, dedicated to his vision. David was off doing his own thing, never interested. Your dad wanted him to be taken care of, but not involved in the business. Without that letter, the trust is just a hidden asset, and David could get away with all this."

Sophia frowned. "What do you mean Dad wanted him to be 'taken care of'? Does David know about this?"

Her mom sighed, swirling the wine in her glass. "Business aside, your dad loved his son. He wanted David to be set, so he planned a payout for him, separate from the company. But you were the one he wanted to lead Grant Technologies."

"And David doesn't know?"

"Not unless he stumbled across the paperwork," her mom said, her expression serious. "But if he did, he'd be going after that trust, not the company. So I don't think he has any clue."

Sophia set down her glass. "And if I can find this letter, I can prove Dad's intentions?"

"Yes," her mom said, a glimmer of hope in her eyes. "And it would show the board that you're the rightful CEO, the one your father wanted to lead the company."

Sophia's thoughts were a whirlwind. "I have to find it, Mom. If I can't, David will destroy everything Dad built."

Her mom reached out, squeezing her hand. "I believe in you, Sophia. And I know your father would be proud. You're stronger than you think."

Sophia nodded, determination hardening her resolve. "I'll find it. I won't let David win."

Her mom smiled sadly. "There's one more thing you should know. The project your dad and Carter's father worked on... it wasn't just business. They wanted to change the world, to create something that would make life better for people. That's why your dad never gave up on it. He believed it could still happen."

Sophia felt a pang in her chest. "So, this was never about money or power for Dad?"

"No," her mom said softly. "It was about making a difference. And I think it's time you made one, too."

Sophia stood up, feeling a new sense of purpose. "I guess I should try to go find that letter."

Her mom gave her a soft look. "Is that it, sweetheart? Feels like there's something *else* on your mind."

Sophia sighed and took a long sip of wine. "I think I did something stupid. I kind of got involved with Carter. He's a damn charmer, that's for sure, and I knew that about him. But then I got caught up in the moment—he showed up at my charity event last night like some knight in shining armor, acting like he actually cared. And I fell for it. I'm so stupid."

Her mom's face softened with pity. "Maybe it's not what it seems, Sophia. Maybe it was real."

Sophia shook her head. "No, Mom. He came into the company to take it over. That was his plan all along. He says he wasn't involved in the David thing, but I'm not so sure now."

"Honey, Carter didn't make David buy those shares and have an affair. David did that all on his own, and that has nothing to do with Carter."

"True, but Carter's been there from the start, trying to take over my company," Sophia insisted, her frustration mounting.

Her mom frowned. "Is the company struggling financially, or were you looking for investors?"

"No," Sophia said, her voice tight. "It came out of nowhere, like he targeted me."

"I'm sure he didn't *target* you, sweetheart. Maybe he just saw an opportunity."

Sophia's eyes flashed with anger. "No, it felt personal. Like this was his plan all along." Her mind was spinning now, the pieces falling together in a way that made her blood boil. "I can't believe I fell for it. *For him*."

Her mom reached across the table, taking her hand gently. "Sweetheart, I know it feels like everything's falling apart right now, but sometimes, when you're caught in the middle of the storm, it's hard to see things clearly."

Sophia took a shaky breath.

"Remember when you first started working at the company?" her mom continued. "You were so young, so determined to prove yourself, but you doubted every decision you made. Your dad used to say you were like a firecracker—bright, fierce, and always ready to explode. But what you needed to learn was how to control that fire, direct it, and not let it burn you up."

Sophia looked down, her mom's words pulling her back to those early days. The long hours, the endless meetings, the constant need to be perfect.

"You've come a long way since then, but I think you still carry some of that fear—that you're not good enough, that people won't see your value. And now, with Carter and David, it's stirring all of that up again. You're questioning yourself, wondering if you've been duped, if you're not as strong as you thought."

Her mom's grip tightened, her voice firm. "But you are strong, Sophia. You've faced tough situations and you always come out on top. This company is in your blood. You don't have to let anyone—Carter, David, or anyone else—take that from you."

Sophia blinked back tears, nodding slowly.

"If Carter lied to you, you'll figure it out. And if there's even a chance that he's being genuine, you'll see that too. But right now, you need to stop reacting and start planning. Be that firecracker, but don't let anyone light your fuse. You decide when and where to explode, okay?"

Sophia took a deep breath, nodding as her mom's words sank in. "So, what you're saying is... I need to stop letting everyone else dictate how I feel. I've been reacting to everything—David's betrayal, Carter's charm, even the board's decisions—like I'm just... I don't know, a passenger in all of this. But I'm not. This is my company, my life. I need to take control and start playing by my own rules."

"Exactly, honey. You've got more power than you realize. Use it."

Sophia nodded again, feeling a new sense of clarity. "I can't keep letting them push me around, second-guessing every move. I need to get ahead of this, find that letter, and remind everyone why I'm the CEO of this company."

"Maybe I just need to go and confront Carter, my brother, and the damn media!" Sophia jumped to her feet, the frustration boiling over. "Expose this whole mess for what it is."

Her mom raised a hand, calm and reliable. "Sophia, sit down for a second. I understand you're upset, but running yourself to the media? That doesn't sound wise. Maybe take a little break, running yourself into the ground won't solve anything."

Sophia's fists clenched. "So what, Mom? I just sit back and let them destroy everything I've worked for? I can't do that. This is my company, my reputation. I need to fight."

"Yes, you need to fight," her mom agreed, "but not at the expense of your sanity. Your dad worked himself to death, and I don't want to see you doing the same. There are more important things in life than just work."

Sophia shook her head. "That's not how you run a company, Mom. You can't just let go. You have to be relentless."

"I watched your father do exactly that, and I watched it kill him," her mom said quietly. "The stress, the endless hours—it consumed him. And now it's doing the same to you. You need to find a balance, or you'll end up exactly where he did."

Sophia paused, the words hitting harder than she expected. "So, what? I just walk away? Let David and Carter win?"

"No, sweetheart. But you need to learn how to let go, how to relax. Maybe this is the universe telling you it's time to take a step back and breathe. You've been running nonstop for years. What has it really brought you? More stress, more pressure, and now this mess."

Sophia crossed her arms defensively. "I'm not just going to sit here and do nothing. I need to find that letter."

"I'm not asking you to do nothing. I'm asking you to take care of yourself. Because, love, you can't pour from an empty cup. The company needs you strong, and so do the people in your life. You're no good to anyone if you're burned out."

Sophia's shoulders sagged as she let out a long breath. "So, what do I do?"

"Go to them, but go with a plan. Don't react. Be the calm, collected leader you are. And think about what's next for you. Is this really how you want to spend your life—fighting every battle like it's the end of the world?"

Sophia sat back down, her mind spinning.

"I'm saying learn to pick your battles. Some things are worth fighting for, and some aren't. You've got to figure out which is which. You've built something incredible, but you need to remember that you're not defined by it. You're more than just this company."

Sophia looked down at her hands, her mother's words sinking in. "You're right. I've been so focused on keeping everything together that I've forgotten to take care of myself."

Her mom smiled softly. "Exactly. You've got this, Sophia, but you need to be smart and take care of yourself first. Then you can handle whatever comes your way."

Sophia nodded. "Okay. One step at a time."

"That's my girl," her mom said, squeezing her hand. "You've got this. Just remember—there's more to life than work." But first Sophia needed to find that letter.

CHAPTER 24

Carter got home, surveying the remnants of last night—No word from her all day. He got the message loud and clear.

After tidying up, he dialed Eleanor. "You should go see Dad," he said when she answered. "They're talking about hospice."

She was quiet for a moment, then let out a shaky breath. "I was afraid of that." She paused, and he could almost picture her rubbing her temple. "I've just been so overwhelmed with the wedding and everything..."

"I can tell." He kept his voice firm. "You're not making great decisions, Eleanor."

She bristled. "What's that supposed to mean?"

"It means this deal with David. It's a mess. He's caught up in some serious trouble—an affair, insider trading, the works. If it gets out, we're all going down with him."

"Are you serious?" Her voice was a mix of disbelief and panic. "How bad is it?"

"Bad. We need to figure this out, fast. I'm not risking everything for some reckless move."

Eleanor sighed heavily. "I just wanted to secure the deal, Carter. With the wedding coming up, I needed this to go smoothly."

"I get that, but you need to see Dad. This might be it." His voice softened. "We can fix the business stuff, but we can't get more time with him."

"I'll go," she said, her tone resigned. "Tomorrow, okay?"

"Okay." He hesitated, then added, "And Eleanor? Just... don't do anything rash."

She let out a dry laugh. "You were right, Carter. I *should* have listened to you."

"I appreciate that," he said, hanging up. He stared at his phone, feeling a heavy mix of worry and frustration.

He went straight to bed and crashed hard. Trying to forget this day.

The next day he barely made it through his morning routine, his head still foggy from the restless night before. By the time he got to the office, he had one clear goal: talk to Sophia and get David out before things spiraled further out of control.

But as he pushed open the door to his office, he froze. Sophia was already there, standing by his desk, her posture tense, eyes blazing with fury. He could feel the anger radiating off her like heat waves.

"Sophia—" he started, but she cut him off, her voice like a whip.

"I came in today to give you a chance, Carter," she said, her tone harsh and unyielding. "But then I ran into your sister this morning."

His stomach dropped. "Eleanor?"

"Yeah, *Eleanor*." Sophia's lips twisted. "She told me I shouldn't be here, that this company was a huge mistake, and you should've been going after a more solid company, not this sinking ship. She made it sound like you zeroed in on my company *specifically*. So, what the hell, Carter? Why *did* you come for Grant Technologies? Why *did* you kick me off as CEO and then pretend to play the nice guy?"

"I didn't—" he began, but she was relentless, her words coming out in a torrent.

"You pretended to care about me, about my company, about my causes, like you were some kind of hero," she spat, her voice shaking. "But you don't give a damn about anything that matters. Not about this company, not about my employees, and certainly not about me. You made me believe you were different. And then you go to lunch with another woman the day after we —" Her voice broke, and she looked away, visibly trying to hold herself together.

"Sophia, it's not like that," Carter said, his voice low and pleading. "I wasn't with anyone else. I'm not trying to hurt you."

"Oh, right," she scoffed, her eyes flashing with anger. "Then tell me why you came for my company, Carter. Why?"

He looked at her. "Look, I wasn't completely honest with you, at first," he said quietly. "I did come for Grant Technologies."

"What are you talking about?" she demanded, her voice sharp with disbelief.

He sank down into his chair. "I did. I'm sorry. Our fathers... They were rivals. I went after your company because of them. But then I got to know you and this company, and my goals changed. I don't want to take you out of this company, Sophia. I'm trying to get you back as CEO."

Her face twisted in hurt and betrayal. "So it *was* personal," she said, her voice cracking. "You did target this company. You lied to me. You made me believe this was just business, but it wasn't."

"Sophia, it wasn't—"

"No!" she cut him off, tears shining in her eyes. "Our dads weren't even rivals, Carter. They were friends. They had a deal go wrong, but my dad kept trying to fix it, to fix their friendship. And now you come along and... oh, what does it matter?" She threw her hands up, her voice breaking. "You don't care. You just told me you came after my company because it was *personal*! You probably set David up to take over, didn't you?"

"No," Carter said, his voice tight. "I had nothing to do with David —"

"Save it!" she shouted, her voice echoing in the room. "This is unforgivable, Carter. You pretended to care. You made me believe you were different. But you're just like everyone else. Worse, even."

She turned and stormed out of the office, wiping tears from her eyes as she went, leaving Carter sitting there, feeling more hollow than he ever thought possible.

CHAPTER 25

Sophia pulled open another dusty file drawer, her movements brisk and frustrated. "Where are you?" she muttered under her breath, rifling through folders of old contracts and memos. She knew it had to be here somewhere—if her dad left a letter, he wouldn't have hidden it far from where he worked day and night.

The fluorescent lights above buzzed, and the empty office seemed even quieter than usual, the silence almost pressing in on her. It was late, the kind of late where only the most desperate or the most dedicated were still at their desks. Sophia knew which category she fell into.

"Come on, Dad, where did you put it?" She ran her fingers along the edges of each folder, searching for anything that felt out of place. Every few minutes, she'd glance at the framed photo on the shelf—her dad beaming at her, the company's name in bold letters behind them. He looked proud. Hopeful.

She shook her head, blinking back the frustration and tears threatening to spill over. "You wanted me to run this company, right? You trusted me. But how am I supposed to do that if I don't have the full picture?"

Pulling out a thick, leather-bound planner, she flipped through the pages, but they were filled with old meeting notes and reminders. She dropped it back in the drawer, slumping. Nothing.

The stack of boxes in the corner caught her eye, and she moved over, pushing one aside to get to another. They were labeled with years and events—1998: New York Office Opening, 2005: Chicago Expansion. She grabbed the one marked 2017, the year her dad had gotten sick. If he'd left something, it would be around then.

She yanked the top off, coughing as dust billowed up. "Yuck," she muttered, waving it away. The box was filled with old marketing plans and budget reports. She flipped through them quickly, each one more useless than the last.

"Where the hell is it?" she groaned, slumping back against the desk. She could feel the panic starting to claw at her. She needed that letter. It could change everything, give her the leverage she needed to push David out and regain control. And more than that, it was the last piece of her father she could hold on to—a confirmation that he believed in her, that he wanted her to lead, not David.

Her phone lit up on the desk, and she glanced at the screen. A text from her mom: *Anything yet?* Sophia typed back quickly, *Still looking. I'll let you know.* She set the phone down, staring at it for a moment, then grabbed another box.

This one was filled with her father's personal belongings. Little trinkets he'd collected over the years, old awards, a couple of framed photos she hadn't seen in ages. She picked one up, smiling softly as she looked at the image of her dad and her, standing outside the office on her first day as CEO. He'd given her a pep talk right before the photo was taken, telling her she could do anything.

"Did you know David was going to do this?" she whispered, her voice cracking. "Did you know he'd try to take everything you built?" She set the picture down carefully and reached deeper into the box.

Her fingers brushed against something smooth and cool—a leather-bound journal, smaller than the rest. She pulled it out, her breath catching as she opened it. Inside were her dad's familiar scrawls, pages of notes, ideas, and at the very back, something that looked like a letter.

She hesitated, her heart pounding in her chest. *Please, please be what I need.*

But as she opened the letter, her heart sank. It was just another set of business notes, ideas he'd had for the company's future, things he'd wanted to implement but never got the chance to. Nothing that could help her now.

She slammed the book shut, her eyes burning with unshed tears. "Damn it!" she hissed, shoving the box away.

Her phone beeped again. This time, it was from Jessica: *Are you okay? I need to talk to you.*

Sophia ignored it, staring at the mess of files and boxes scattered around her. She was running out of places to look, running out of time. If she didn't find something soon, David would cement his position, and she'd lose the company for good.

She squared her shoulders, determination hardening her resolve. She was going to find that letter, but for now, it was a dead end. Shifting gears, she focused on what she could control —getting the board on her side and proving she was still the right person to lead Grant Technologies, no matter what David had been saying behind her back.

By the time she got home it was late. She was exhausted but resolute. The next day, she set up a series of meetings, starting with Jonathan Avery, a long-time board member and an old friend of her father's. If anyone would be willing to listen, it would be him.

Jonathan greeted her with a tight smile as she stepped into his office, the faint scent of cigars and polished wood hanging over him. "Sophia, it's good to see you," he said, gesturing for her to sit. "I was surprised to get your call."

"I'm sure you were." She took a seat, smoothing her skirt over her knees. "I'm hoping we can talk about what's happening with the company. I think there's been a lot of misinformation going around."

Jonathan's eyes flickered, his expression guarded. "Yes, I've heard quite a bit, actually."

"Look, Jonathan, I know things have been chaotic lately, but I want to assure you that I'm committed to this company, just like my father was. David has no experience, no vision for the future. I need to know if I can count on your support to take back the CEO position."

He leaned back. "I want to believe in you, Sophia, but the board is concerned. There are... rumors."

Sophia frowned. "Rumors? What kind of rumors?"

Jonathan hesitated, his fingers tapping lightly on the arm of his chair. "I don't want to get into specifics, but let's just say there are questions about your leadership—about whether you're fit to run the company."

"What are you talking about?" Her frustration bubbled to the surface. "Jonathan, you've known me since I was a kid. I've dedicated my entire life to this company. What's changed?"

He sighed, rubbing his temples. "It's not just about your work, Sophia. There's talk of... personal issues. Financial troubles. Something about an affair?"

Sophia's heart stopped. "An affair? Financial troubles?" She shook her head, trying to process what he was saying. "None of that is true. Who's spreading this garbage?"

Jonathan shrugged helplessly. "I don't know, but it's out there. And it's making people nervous. They think the company needs stability, and right now, you're not providing that."

"Jonathan, I swear to you, those rumors are false. David is the one with problems, not me. He's the one with the debts, the personal issues. He's not fit to lead."

"I hope you can prove that, Sophia. But until you do, I'm afraid I can't stick my neck out for you." He shifted forward, his voice softer. "I'm sorry."

She left Jonathan's office feeling like she'd been punched. If even he was doubting her, she was in more trouble than she thought.

Her next stop was to see Diane Mitchell, one of the newer board members. Diane had always been vocal about wanting a strong female leader at the helm of the company.

But Diane's office was just as cold as Jonathan's had been. "Sophia," she greeted, her voice neutral as she offered a seat.

"Diane, I won't waste your time. I'm here to ask for your support in removing David from the CEO position and reinstating me."

Diane's lips tightened. "I've always been a supporter of women in leadership, but the board is worried, Sophia. There are rumors..."

Sophia's stomach twisted. **Rumors, again.** Every meeting, it was the same. Each board member seemed to have a different version of the story, but they all pointed at her. Financial problems. An affair. The details were blurry and inconsistent, but the damage was the same. Doubt. Distrust. And David? Not a single mention of his debts, his scandalous behavior, or his lack of experience. It was all on her.

Back in her office, she slammed the door and rested against it, staring blankly at the sleek, modern decor that now felt cold and uninviting. How could they believe all this nonsense? She'd been at this company for years, proving herself time and again, and now, they were willing to throw her away because of a few whispered lies.

She dropped into her chair, her mind racing. David. He had to be behind this. Spreading rumors, twisting the narrative. And Carter and Eleanor, no doubt, were in on it too. It was all part of their plan to make her look like the problem while David swooped in to "save" the company.

Sophia's phone chimed, breaking through her chaotic thoughts. She glanced at the screen—an email from Emily, an old college friend she hadn't spoken to in years. The subject line read: *Not sure you saw this—Is everything OK?*

Her heart sank as she opened it.

> *Hey Soph, just wanted to reach out. Saw this article and was shocked. Is this true? Is everything okay over there? Let me know if you need to talk. Take care.*

The message was short, but the link attached hit her like a brick. She clicked on it, and a glaring headline blazed across the screen:

"Grant Technologies in Crisis: Mismanagement, Scandals, and a CEO in Over Her Head?"

Her stomach twisted as she skimmed through the article. Words like *turmoil*, *questionable ethics*, and *board unrest* jumped out at her. They'd painted her as an incompetent leader, hinting at mismanagement and chaos behind closed doors. There were even insinuations of financial instability and rumors of inappropriate relationships affecting her decision-making.

It was a hatchet job, through and through. And worse, it was filled with enough half-truths to seem credible to anyone who didn't know better. Her eyes flicked over to a line that stood out like a neon sign:

"Sources close to the company suggest that personal conflicts and poor leadership have led to this internal crisis, with some board members already considering drastic changes."

Sophia's chest tightened as she read on. The article speculated about layoffs, department closures, even a possible merger or sale. There were quotes from anonymous "insiders" hinting that her leadership was the root of the problem, that the company was "in need of stronger, more experienced management."

She felt her face flush with anger. Stronger, more experienced management. Like David, no doubt. The whole thing reeked of his manipulation.

A notification popped up—more messages, more emails. The floodgates had opened, and she knew she'd spend the next few hours fending off questions and trying to put out fires she hadn't even seen coming.

Who else had David turned against her? And Carter—had he been in on this? He was part of the problem, whether he admitted it or not. She can't believe she trusted him.

But she needed to be smart. She had to find that letter. If she could prove her father's wishes and show the board she was the rightful CEO, she could stop this takeover in its tracks. Or had the damage already been done?

Sophia glanced around her office, trying to think. Where would her dad have kept something so important? She'd already gone through everything at home, at the office. The archives were clean too. What was she missing?

And then it hit her. His old study. The one at the lake house they used to visit every summer when she was a kid. The house had been turned into a seasonal rental after her dad got sick, but he'd spent hours in that study—going through old files, reading, writing.

It was a long shot, but if there was anywhere left to search, it was there.

Another notification lit up her phone. It was Tricia, one of the board members from her Alzheimer's nonprofit.

Sophia, the numbers are in from the gala. We got a $10 million *donation!*

Sophia stared at the message. *Ten million*? That was bigger than all their previous years combined. She quickly dialed Tricia's number.

"Tricia, what? Ten million? That's incredible!" Sophia couldn't keep the shock out of her voice. "Who made the donation?"

"It's unbelievable, right?" Tricia's excitement buzzed through the line. "It looks like it was made in the name of Richard Kane."

Sophia's heart stopped. Richard Kane? As in Carter's father?

"Richard Kane?" she echoed, trying to keep her voice steady. "Are you sure?"

"Yeah, it's all in the paperwork," Tricia confirmed. "I've got to run to a meeting, but I'll send you more details later."

"Okay, thanks, Tricia," Sophia said, still dazed as she hung up. Why would Richard Kane be donating to her charity?

Focus, Sophia. One thing at a time. Grabbing her things, she dialed her mom as she headed to her car.

"Hey, Mom, is the spare key still at the lake house?"

"Yes, but it's shut down for the season," her mom replied, a note of caution in her voice. "We only rent it out in the summer now."

"I know," Sophia said. "But aren't some of Dad's old files in the back storage? I was thinking the letter might be there. Maybe in one of the books or something."

Her mom hesitated. "His old desk is still in the study, but everything's been cleaned out. It's just a rental now, Sophia. Most of the furniture is for show."

"I have to try, Mom. It's the only place I can think of."

There was a pause. "Okay, well, it's a two-hour drive, but the key's in the usual spot. Just be careful, alright?"

"I will, thanks." Sophia hung up and threw her bag into the passenger seat.

Starting the car, she made a mental note to look into Richard Kane later. Wow, 10 million?

Her phone rang, Carter's name flashing on the screen. Without hesitation, she sent it straight to voicemail. A moment later, a text notification popped up.

Sophia, I saw the article. I'm so sorry. This is my fault. I never wanted it to get this far. I know you're hurting, and I don't blame you for being angry. But please believe me, I'm trying to fix this. You mean more to me than this deal ever did.

Sophia let out a bitter laugh and tossed the phone onto the passenger seat. "Lies," she muttered, gripping the steering wheel until her knuckles turned white. "All lies." He is just like Evan.

The city blurred past her as she sped onto the highway.

CHAPTER 26

Carter's stomach churned as he navigated the winding road to Uncle Bruce's place. He'd arranged to drop by, hoping for some clarity about those pictures. The image of his dad and James Grant together—smiling, looking like friends—kept flashing in his mind, conflicting with everything he'd ever known.

Sophia's words echoed too. "Our dads weren't rivals, they were friends." What if everything he thought he knew was wrong?

He shook his head, gripping the steering wheel. All he'd ever been told was that James Grant had screwed his father over, going behind his back on a deal. He remembered how, after that, his dad had spiraled—his business gone, his mind unraveling. That betrayal had been the fuel for so much of Carter's life, pushing him to prove himself, to win at any cost.

And then came Grant Technologies, like a prize served up on a silver platter. The timing had seemed perfect, and he'd thought taking down that company would feel like justice. But now, all he felt was regret. Even more so after seeing Sophia fight like hell to protect what her father had built. Smart, fierce, and genuinely good.

He glanced at his phone again, Blake's forwarded email glaring at him. The article was brutal, a vicious takedown of Sophia's leadership. False rumors about affairs and financial mismanagement—all aimed at her. It had David written all over it. Or was it Eleanor, trying to salvage the mess they'd created?

He'd tried calling Sophia, but she wasn't picking up. After he sent the text, he'd stared at his phone, hoping she'd respond, even just to yell at him. But nothing.

"Fix it," he muttered to himself. He wasn't the type to sit back and do nothing, but that's exactly what he'd been doing, watching as everything fell apart. That was over. He'd made a mess, and now he needed to start cleaning it up. Sophia deserved that much.

The car crested a hill, and Uncle Bruce's old, sprawling farmhouse came into view. Time to dig into the past and figure out what the hell really happened between their fathers.

Uncle Bruce looked older than the last time Carter had seen him—grayer and more stooped, but still sturdy enough to get around. He met Carter at the door, a gruff smile on his face, and pulled him into a surprisingly strong hug. There was a faint but persistent cough, a reminder of age and time.

"Carter, you old dog," Bruce rumbled, clapping him on the back. "Didn't expect to see you here. What brings you out to my neck of the woods?"

"Just need some clarity on something," Carter said, stepping back. "I don't have a lot of time, but I saw some old pictures at the nursing home, and I wanted to talk to you about them. Specifically, about James Grant."

Bruce's face tightened for a moment, then he nodded and waved Carter inside. The house was just as he remembered—cozy but cluttered, with the faint smell of tobacco and old wood. They sat at the worn kitchen table, a couple of chipped mugs between them.

"So, James Grant, huh?" Bruce reclined back, his expression thoughtful. "I always thought your dad made too much of that mess. James wasn't the bad guy he made him out to be. They were close, you know, almost like brothers."

Carter's stomach twisted. "Dad always said James went behind his back on a deal."

Bruce snorted. "Sure, something went wrong, but it wasn't like James did it on purpose. They had a project together —Complicated stuff. The funding fell through, and your dad blamed James for pulling out, but it wasn't really his fault. Things just... fell apart. Your dad couldn't handle that. Got all wrapped up in revenge, thinking James betrayed him. It was his downfall, you know. The obsession. He lost it all—money, business, everything." Maybe he was following in his father's footsteps after all. Letting revenge ruin him.

Carter hunched forward, every word driving home the realization that he'd been operating on the wrong set of facts. "So, they didn't hate each other?"

Bruce shook his head, his cough breaking up his words. "Nah, not really. Sure, your dad was angry, but James tried to make amends. Sent him a letter, apologizing for how it all went down. Even outlined how he kept working on the project and developed a trust and a patent. But by then, your dad's memory was starting to go. I think he just... forgot about the whole thing."

Carter's heart pounded. "Do you know what happened to the letter?"

Bruce scratched his chin, thinking. "If I had to guess, it's probably still with your dad at the nursing home. He kept all his important stuff with him after he moved in. But hell, he might not even remember it exists."

Carter stood up, feeling a strange mix of relief and urgency. "Thanks, Uncle Bruce. I'm going to head over there now."

Bruce gave him a knowing look. "Good luck, kid. Sometimes, finding the past is the only way to fix the future."

Carter nodded but before he could go digging through his dad's things, there was something else he had to take care of first. Something that had been gnawing at him all day.

He pulled out his phone, quickly tapping out a text to his assistant: *Cancel all my meetings this afternoon. I'm taking care of something urgent.*

He climbed into his truck, still driving it despite splurging on a fancy car that now gave him buyer's remorse. He was done chasing the things that had been his father's downfall—revenge and empty status symbols. It was time to focus on what really mattered. Instead of heading back toward the city, he turned onto a winding road in the opposite direction. He knew exactly where he was going.

CHAPTER 27

The lake house felt more musty than she remembered, a thick, dusty scent lingering in the air, as if it had been sitting alone and empty for too long. She took a deep breath, letting the familiar mix of cedar and lake water wash over her. Despite its neglect, the place still held a certain charm. It was beautiful, really—a perfect rental now. But it was so much more than that.

She wandered through the hallway, her fingers trailing along the rough wooden walls. As a kid, this had been her paradise. Lazy summer days spent swimming in the lake, running barefoot through the garden, staying up late to catch fireflies with David. They'd been close once. So close.

A memory floated to the surface, clear and painful: the two of them, maybe ten and twelve, splashing each other in the shallow water while their dad grilled on the deck and their mom sang along to some old Beatles song. They'd been a happy family then, before everything got complicated. Before ambition and resentment carved deep, unbridgeable gaps between them.

She shook her head, finding the spare key under the porch mat and sliding it into the lock. Inside, the house was different now —stripped of its old, familiar clutter, everything arranged just so for renters who probably didn't know the stories the walls held. But the view through the wide glass windows was the same, and it still took her breath away. The lake stretched out in a serene, endless blue, the light glinting off the water like scattered diamonds.

How had she forgotten how much she loved this place? She'd

dreamed of living here one day, relaxing on the deck with a book and a glass of wine, maybe even raising her own family here. But when was the last time she'd actually relaxed? Oh, right— the night she spent with Carter. That had been something else entirely. One perfect night, so different from the chaos that had followed.

She sighed, pushing the thought away. Why did he have to turn out to be her worst nightmare?

With a determined breath, she headed straight to the study, her gaze sweeping over the shelves lined with old, decorative books. She pulled them down one by one, flipping through pages that no one had touched in years. Nothing. Moving on to the desk, she checked every drawer, felt underneath for a hidden compartment. Her fingers brushed against smooth wood, then an uneven groove. She hesitated, pressing on it, but nothing happened. Damn.

She settled back. This was ridiculous. She was hunting for a ghost, chasing something that might not even exist, all because of a hunch. Two hours away for no reason at all. Maybe she just needed an escape.

Her phone beeped in her pocket, the pull of habit making her reach for it. The instinct to log into work, to respond to emails, was strong, almost automatic. And look where that had gotten her. Fired. Betrayed. Her reputation shredded. She'd thought she was doing the right thing, leading the company forward, helping people, making a difference. And now? Now she was here, at this empty lake house, looking for a last-ditch lifeline.

Maybe the universe was telling her it was time to let go of that life and find something simpler. This one didn't seem so bad. The quiet, the solitude, the slow pace. Why hadn't she come here more often? Because she'd been too busy chasing a dream that wasn't even hers anymore.

Her dad had warned her not to work herself to death. He'd lived it, sacrificing everything for success, only to lose what mattered most. Was she doing the same thing?

She sank down into the old armchair, the leather cool and cracked beneath her fingers. Was this really the life she wanted? Running herself ragged, chasing goals that seemed to dissolve the closer she got? She'd been fooled by the wrong guy, pushed out of the company she'd given everything to, and for what?

Maybe she'd been fighting for the wrong things. Maybe it was time to start over, to live a life that didn't revolve around board meetings and corporate takeovers. But damn, she still wanted to save her dad's company. She owed him that much.

But if she didn't find this letter... then what?

Sophia stared at her reflection in the old mirror, the dark circles under her eyes betraying just how exhausted she felt. She was fighting battles on all fronts, and it showed. Would she even recognize herself anymore if she managed to save the company? Or would she be a shell of the person she used to be?

She sighed, feeling the fatigue deep in her bones. Maybe a nap would clear her head. Just a few minutes to shut her eyes and escape from the weight pressing down on her. She stretched out on the old sofa in the study, the cushions stiff and unyielding but familiar. Her eyes drifted closed almost immediately, the sound of the lake outside soothing her into a deep, dreamless sleep.

When she finally woke up, two hours had passed, and the room was bathed in the soft light of the setting sun. Groggy and disoriented, she sat up, blinking away the remnants of sleep. For a moment, she couldn't remember where she was. Then the view through the windows—the lake shimmering in the evening light —reminded her.

The lake house. The letter. Her father.

Her phone flashed insistently on the coffee table. She picked it up and winced at the screen: dozens of missed calls, a flood of texts.

Probably all about that damn article. Heat flushed her cheeks. How could things have gotten so out of control?

As if on cue, her phone rang again, the screen lighting up with her mom's name. She took a deep breath and answered, trying to sound awake

"Hi, Mom."

"Honey, are you okay?" Her mother's voice was thick with concern.

Sophia rubbed her eyes, trying to shake off the grogginess as her mom's words registered. "Did you see it?"

"See what, Mom?" she asked, confused.

"Did you see what Carter said?"

"What are you talking about?"

Her mom paused for a second, then said, "Hold on, I'm sending you a link."

Her phone gave a quick alert. She clicked on it, and a video popped up—posted about two hours ago with thousands of views already. It was a press statement from Carter.

She hesitated, then hit play.

Carter's face filled the screen, serious and sincere. He spoke directly to the camera.

"I want to address the rumors and recent articles surrounding Grant Technologies and its leadership," he began. "There have been false claims suggesting unethical behavior within the company. I'm here to say, unequivocally, that these rumors do not involve Sophia Grant."

Sophia's breath caught as he continued.

"Sophia is a leader of integrity, strength, and vision," Carter said. "She has dedicated her career to upholding the values her father instilled in Grant Technologies. James Grant was a good man who built a solid foundation for this company."

He paused, his eyes softening. "Under her leadership, Grant Technologies has not only thrived but has also made significant strides in innovation, community engagement, and employee welfare. Initiatives like the new family leave policy and the development of the eco-friendly product line were all spearheaded by her."

Sophia felt a lump form in her throat. How did he even know all that?

Carter took a deep breath before continuing. "I'll be honest —when I first considered acquiring Grant Technologies, my intentions weren't pure. I saw it as an opportunity to settle old scores, and that's on me. But as I got to know Sophia and the company she's built, my perspective changed completely."

The interviewer's voice cut in, a skeptical note in her tone. "Backing Sophia publicly could have serious repercussions for Kane Enterprises. Are you prepared for the potential backlash?"

Carter's response was immediate, firm. "If supporting Sophia and the work she's doing has consequences, then so be it. If my board can't see what a beautiful, impactful company Grant Technologies is under her leadership, that's their loss. We would be honored to partner with her."

The video ended, leaving Sophia staring at her phone, stunned.

"Did you hear all that?" her mom asked gently. "He really stuck his neck out for you."

Sophia swallowed hard. "Yeah... yeah, I did."

"Sweetie, maybe it's not what you think. Maybe Carter's trying to —"

"I don't know, Mom," Sophia interrupted, her voice shaky. "I just... I don't know what to believe anymore."

But as she stood there, still holding her phone, a new thought began to take root. Maybe, just maybe, Carter *was* trying to make things right.

"Thanks for sending this to me, Mom." Sophia felt a strange mix of emotions swirling in her chest—relief, confusion, and something that felt uncomfortably close to hope.

Her mom hesitated. "Honey, there's something else I need to tell you. I heard from David."

Sophia's heart dropped. "What now? Did he come up with another scheme?"

"No, it's the opposite," her mom said, her voice cautious. "He's stepping down as CEO."

"What?" Sophia blinked, completely thrown. "Why?"

"Apparently, an anonymous source paid off his debts. He's... well, not interested in being a CEO anymore."

"Who would do that?"

Her mom was quiet for a moment. "I think we both know who."

Sophia's grip tightened around her phone. Carter. It had to be him. He'd just defended her publicly, risking his own reputation, and now this? He'd bought David out.

"Mom, I... I don't know what to say." She felt the words tangling, a mixture of gratitude and frustration. Gratitude that someone was trying to help, frustration that she'd needed the help in the first place.

"Maybe he's not the enemy you think he is. Maybe he's been telling the truth."

Sophia stared out at the lake, her thoughts knotted. "I need to talk to him," Sophia murmured, more to herself than to her mom.

She took a deep breath lingering on the serene lake as she tried to sort through the chaos in her mind. Carter's press statement, David stepping down, the mysterious donation by Richard Kane. She needed to talk to Carter, but first, she needed to clear her head.

Something was nagging at her, something she'd been meaning to do since Tricia mentioned it. That donation... Richard Kane. Why would he donate such a huge amount?

She pulled out her phone and quickly googled his name. The founder of Kane Enterprises but not much more. There wasn't much—just a few vague business mentions and an address. The location wasn't far from her place. What could she possibly say to him? Why did you donate to my charity? Did you know my dad? It felt ridiculous, but it was eating her up. Ten million was worth a personal thank you.

Before she could second-guess herself, Sophia grabbed her bag. It was a retirement center. But she had to know. For her dad. For herself.

Sophia took a deep breath, clutching her bag as she pushed through the doors of the retirement home. The air smelled like a mix of sterility and attempted comfort. She approached the front desk.

"Hi, I'm looking for Richard Kane."

The receptionist, a kind-looking woman with glasses perched on her nose, glanced at the clock on the wall. "It's a bit late, but he's still up. It's good he's getting visitors—he may not have much time left." She offered a sympathetic smile. "Right this way."

Sophia nodded, swallowing hard as she followed the woman down a series of quiet, dimly lit hallways. Was she really doing this? What did she expect to find? She pushed the thoughts aside, focusing instead on the steady click of her heels against the linoleum floor.

Finally, they reached a small room at the end of the hall. The door was slightly ajar, and as Sophia stepped inside, she froze. There, sitting beside the bed, was Carter. He looked up, his expression equally shocked to see her.

"What are you doing here?" she asked, her voice barely above a whisper.

He stood up, surprise flickering across his face. "What are *you* doing here?"

She glanced past him to the frail man in the chair, who looked so fragile, his eyes distant and unseeing. "I came to talk to Richard Kane... and—oh my God." The realization hit her like a wave. "Of course, he's your dad. This makes sense now, and... I'm so sorry."

Carter crossed the room in a few quick steps, his presence overwhelming. Without thinking, she stepped into his embrace, his arms wrapping around her like a lifeline.

"No, I'm sorry," he murmured against her hair. He pulled back slightly, looking down at her. "But really, *why are you here?*"

She took a deep breath, glancing at Richard again. "Your dad made a huge donation to my charity, and I wanted to thank him personally. I didn't realize..."

"That was from me," Carter interrupted gently, his eyes soft.

"Why?" she asked, confused.

He glanced back at his father, his voice thick with emotion. "Because he has Alzheimer's, and it's... it's been rough. I wanted to do something that mattered, something that might help people like him."

Sophia's heart clenched as she saw the pain etched across his face. "Thank you, Carter. That means more than you know. I really didn't know."

He nodded, his gaze never leaving hers. "I didn't mean for any of this to happen, Sophia. I'm trying to fix it, but..."

She cut him off gently, squeezing his hand. "I know." They stood in silence for a moment, the air thick with unspoken words.

For the first time, she saw past the businessman, the rival, the enemy. She saw the man beneath, struggling with his own battles, trying to find a way to make things right.

"Why didn't you tell me?" she asked softly.

"About my dad?" His voice was hoarse. "I don't know. I guess I didn't want you to see me as weak."

She shook her head. "Carter, that's not weakness. That's... it's *human*."

He gave her a small, grateful smile. "I don't know how much time I have left with him, so I'm spending it here as much as I can."

She nodded, the weight of his words sinking in. "Is it okay that I'm here?"

"Yes," he said, his voice softening. "You lighten up the space."

Sophia glanced around the room, taking in the sterile walls, before looking back at Carter. She sat down beside him, finding unexpected comfort in his presence in such a vulnerable place. For a moment, neither of them spoke, letting the quiet settle between them. Then, as if on cue, they both started talking at once.

"Thank you," she said, her voice overlapping with his.

"Thank you for everything," she continued, as he said, "You have your company back, and I'll gladly walk away if that's what it takes. I never meant to hurt you."

Sophia looked at him, her heart aching with a mix of gratitude and regret. "Maybe I needed this wake-up call. I've been working myself ragged for so long, but for what? We should be spending time with the people we love, right?"

He smiled, a hint of sadness in his eyes. "Right."

"Let's talk business tomorrow," he added. "I'm not sure I have it in me to discuss it right now. Just know that I'll walk away, regardless of the consequences."

She drifted to the piece of paper in his hand. "What's that?"

Carter glanced down at the folded letter, almost as if he'd forgotten he was holding it. "Well, perfect timing. I found this old letter from your dad, actually. You were right—they were friends."

Sophia blinked. "Are you serious? The universe has a funny sense of humor, doesn't it?" She took the letter, her eyes scanning her dad's handwriting. It was unmistakably her father's.

"Can I read it?" she asked, her voice barely above a whisper.

"Of course," he said, leaning back, giving her space.

"You can read it out loud if you want," Carter said softly.

Sophia nodded, unfolding the letter. She took a deep breath and began to read.

"Dear Richard,

I hope this letter finds you well. I've been thinking a lot about our partnership, and I want to say how deeply sorry I am that things went south the way they did. I know we both had high hopes, and I take responsibility for my part in how it ended. But I still believe in what we were building together.

I wanted you to know that I've been working on our project these past few years. It's finally finished, and I've filed a patent. Along with the patent documents, you'll find a trust outlining ownership. It wasn't easy, but I pushed through because I knew it was something we both believed in—something that could change lives. I couldn't let it go, knowing how much it meant to both of us.

I would like to launch it, but only with your approval and only as partners—just like we always planned. I've missed working with you, but more than that, I've missed our friendship. You've always been more than just a business partner to me, Rich. You're my dear friend, and I will always cherish the memories we've made.

Please, think about it. I know things didn't end well, but I'm hoping this can be a new beginning for both of us.

Yours, always,

James"

Sophia's voice cracked on the last word, tears spilling down her cheeks. She glanced at Carter, her heart aching with a mix of sorrow and disbelief. "It wasn't the letter I thought, but that's okay. They weren't enemies—they were friends. My dad was trying to make things right."

Carter nodded, his own eyes shimmering with unshed tears. "I didn't know. I thought… I thought they hated each other."

She wiped her face with the back of her hand, holding the letter close. "What happened to the patent?"

"I don't know," Carter said honestly.

Sophia glanced down at the letter again. "Maybe we can find it."

"Whatever you need, I'm here to help," Carter said softly, his hand hovering near hers. Before Sophia could respond, a faint murmur from across the room made them both turn.

"James?" Richard Kane's voice, weak but clear, cut through the silence. Carter's head snapped around, eyes wide with shock.

"Dad?" he said, his voice catching. He eased forward, not daring to believe what he was hearing. "Dad, did you just say James?"

Richard blinked, as if coming out of a fog, his heavy eyes finding Carter's. "Son… Is James here?"

Carter's heart clenched, emotions swirling. He glanced at Sophia, who looked just as stunned. "No, Dad. But his daughter is. This is Sophia."

Richard's eyes drifted to Sophia, a soft smile spreading across his face. "Well, aren't you beautiful? You've got James's eyes."

Sophia's heart swelled, tears brimming as she managed a smile. "Thank you, Mr. Kane."

Richard nodded slowly, his smile widening as if he were recalling a fond memory. "I gave him my approval years ago. Told him to go ahead. It was our dream, you know. Both of ours."

Carter leaned in, disbelief and hope warring on his face. "You knew? You gave him your approval?"

But before Richard could respond, his eyes clouded over, his focus drifting away as the brief moment of clarity faded. He seemed lost again, confusion settling back over his features.

Carter sat back, his heart pounding. "Wow. That's the most lucid he's been in ages," he whispered, his voice thick with emotion. "I needed that."

Sophia reached out, her fingers brushing against his. "So did I," she said softly, her heart aching with the bittersweetness of it all. For a moment, it felt like everything might just fall into place.

Sophia's hand lingered on his, the connection between them electric. Carter looked at her, his face intense, searching her eyes as if trying to find the right words. Then, without warning, he sank in, his lips brushing against hers with a tenderness that made her heart stop.

"Sophia," he murmured against her lips, "will you have dinner with me tonight?"

She pulled back just enough to meet his eyes, her heart

fluttering. For a moment, she hesitated, thinking of everything that had happened, but the sincerity in his eyes made the decision for her.

"I would love to," she whispered, a smile spreading across her face.

Carter's thumb brushed over her cheek as he held her blue eyes, his voice low and earnest. "Promise me you won't leave in the morning."

Sophia raised an eyebrow. "Wow, that was presumptuous."

He paused, a faint blush creeping up his neck. "I just meant... I don't want you to feel like you have to run off again."

Sophia chuckled softly, her eyes softening as she looked at him. "I know what you meant."

Carter hesitated, then added, "By the way, that woman who showed up for lunch? I told her I was already seeing someone special."

Sophia's expression shifted, surprise mingling with something warmer. "You did?"

He nodded, his eyes never leaving hers. "I did. Because I am. And I didn't want there to be any confusion."

Her heart swelled, a mix of emotions swirling inside her—relief, happiness, and hope. "I guess that's good to know," she said lightly, but her voice betrayed how much it meant to her.

Carter leaned in, his forehead resting against hers. "I meant what I said, Sophia. I'm not going anywhere." He pressed another soft kiss to her lips, his hand still gently cradling her face. "So... dinner?"

Sophia laughed, the sound light and genuine. "Dinner sounds perfect."

Her phone buzzed, breaking the quiet moment. She glanced at

the screen—Jessica. She sent it straight to voicemail, but almost immediately, a text notification popped up.

Sophia, I told you we need to talk! I need to make up for what I did. Your brother found a patent that I think you should know about.

Sophia's eyebrows shot up as she read the message. The missing patent? She quickly typed back: *Thanks, Jessica. Meet me in my office tomorrow. I'll be in late.*

Carter watched her, curiosity in his eyes. "Who was that?"

She took a breath, her mind spinning with the implications. "Looks like the missing patent has been found."

Carter's eyebrows rose. "Don't you want to call her?"

Sophia shook her head, slipping her phone back into her bag. "Tonight, work can wait."

A smile spread across Carter's face, genuine and warm. "It most definitely can."

She smiled back, the tension of the past few days easing, just for a moment. "So, where are we going for dinner?" she asked, leaning into him.

Epilogue

A few months later

Carter shifted back in his chair, stretching his arms before glancing over at Sophia, who was deep into her documents. "You know," he began, a smirk on his lips, "now that we've merged our companies and that patent has revolutionized how we do things... will you even *have* work to do, Sophia?"

She glanced up with a laugh. "Trust me, running two companies will keep me plenty busy. But I've been thinking... How about we renovate this place and make it our home?"

His eyebrows lifted in surprise, a grin spreading across his face. "What about work?"

She tilted her head, giving him a playful look. "Ever heard of *work from home*?"

He chuckled, looking around at the cozy space, the lake shimmering just beyond the window. "I think it's a brilliant idea."

Sophia smiled. "So, what are *you* going to do now that I'm CEO of both companies?"

Carter leaned back, a thoughtful grin crossing his face. "Actually, there's a certain board position at your charity that I've got my eye on."

She raised an eyebrow, amused. "Really? You want to join the board?"

"Well," he said, smirking, "you'll need someone to keep an eye on those donation numbers. Plus, it seems like a good way to stay involved while you're conquering the corporate world."

She laughed. "Alright, I'll make a few calls. I *think* we can find a spot for you." She winked at him.

Before Sophia could continue, a new alert blinked onto the

display. She glanced at the screen and smiled. "It's my mom. Give me a second." She answered the call, her voice warm. "Hey, Mom!"

"I just wanted to say how thrilled I am that you're renovating the place," her mom gushed. "It's going to be beautiful, and I'm so glad you decided to buy it."

"Thanks, Mom," Sophia replied softly, touched by the sentiment. "And thank you for letting me take it off your hands."

Her mom hesitated. "Actually, there's someone here who wants to say something." There was a muffled sound as the phone was passed over, and then a voice Sophia hadn't heard in months came through the line.

"Sophia... it's me, David."

She froze, surprise and a tangle of emotions flooding her. "David?"

"Look... I'm so sorry for everything," he said, his voice cracking. "I got in over my head, and I've spent the last few months getting clean and getting my head straight. I know I've messed up, but I hope you can forgive me."

Sophia blinked back the sudden sting of tears. "Time heals all wounds, David. Thank you for saying that. I'm glad you're doing better."

There was a pause, then a soft, relieved sigh from her brother. "Thanks, Soph. It means a lot."

"Take care, David," she said softly. "And tell Mom I'll call her later."

"Will do," he replied before the line went dead.

Sophia set her phone down, feeling a little lighter. Just as she did, a knock at the door pulled her back to the present. Eleanor stepped inside, looking every bit the glowing bride. "Sorry I've been such a bridezilla these last few months," she said with a sheepish smile. "It's been... a lot."

Sophia laughed as Eleanor pulled her into a hug. "You're fine. Not a total B."

"Just a partial B," Carter teased, dodging a light smack from his sister.

"Thanks for letting Eleanor use the lake house for the wedding," Carter added, glancing at Sophia.

"No problem," Sophia replied with a smile.

Eleanor, her eyes shining with excitement, looked around. "Okay, where's Dad? He was cleared to walk me down the aisle, right?"

Sophia nodded. "He's ready."

Eleanor's smile softened as she took a deep breath. "I can't believe it. You've done so much for him. We've really seen an improvement in Dad since he started that program you suggested."

Carter added, his tone serious. "We wouldn't have known about it if not for you."

A moment later, the door opened again, and Jessica walked in, beaming. "Am I too late?"

Sophia shook her head, grinning. "You're right on time."

Later, as the sun dipped beneath the horizon, the wedding ceremony unfolded beautifully. Eleanor, glowing in her gown, stood proudly beside Kyle, who had a warm, proud smile as he held her arm.

After the vows, Eleanor turned, bouquet in hand, and tossed it high into the air. Time slowed as it spun, and with a soft thud, it landed right in Sophia's hands.

The End